JOHN'S FIGHT WITH THE BEAR. Page 79.

THE
FRONTIER SERIES
Illustrated
PLANTING
THE
WILDERNESS
BOSTON
LEE & SHEPARD.

THE FRONTIER SERIES.

PLANTING THE WILDERNESS;

OR,

THE PIONEER BOYS.

A STORY OF FRONTIER LIFE.

BY

JAMES D. McCABE, (JR.)

BOSTON:
LEE AND SHEPARD.
1870.

ELECTROTYPED AT THE
BOSTON STEREOTYPE FOUNDRY,
19 Spring Lane.

PREFACE.

THE author has endeavored to present in these pages a faithful picture of the life and trials of those brave men and women who drove out the savage from the great West, and laid the foundations of that mighty empire, of which we Americans of to-day are justly so proud. This portion of our history has been too much neglected, and it is hoped that this little work will induce many a young American to inform himself of the events of that part of our country's career which we call our pioneer history. It is believed that the picture presented herein is "true to life," for, although the characters are fictitious, the incidents related are based upon actual occurrences, and there are persons still living in the Ohio valley, who can testify to the general truthfulness of the narrative.

J. D. McC., JR.

NEW YORK, October, 1, 1869.

THE FRONTIER SERIES.

FOUR VOLUMES, ILLUSTRATED.

---

1. ***The Cabin on the Prairie.*** By Rev. C. H. Pearson. Price $1.25.

2. ***Planting the Wilderness;*** or, The Pioneer Boys. By J. D. McCabe. Price $1.25.

3. ***A Thousand Miles' Walk Across South America.*** By Nathaniel H. Bishop. Price $1.50.

4. ***Twelve Nights in the Hunters' Camp.*** By Rev. Wm. Barrows. Price $1.25.

CONTENTS.

PLANTING THE WILDERNESS.

CHAPTER I.

LEAVING THE OLD HOME.

In the early spring of the year of our Lord 1773, there lived on the Upper Potomac, in the County of Loudon, in the then Colony of Virginia, a man by the name of Thomas Oxenford. He was a plain, honest, God-fearing man, and was forty-four years old. He was of English descent, and his parents had come originally to Alexandria, from which place they had removed to the County of Loudon, and had settled upon a small farm, not far from where the town of Leesburg now stands. Thomas Oxenford was an only child, and, consequently, had inherited the little property of his parents, who had died in his thirtieth year; but this property, which consisted of a tolerably stocked farm of two hundred acres of medium quality land, had also come to him heavily encumbered by his father's debts, and it proved, in the end, as much of a burden as a profit.

Mr. Oxenford had married about a year previous to the death of his father, his last surviving parent, and, at the time of which I write, his family consisted of himself and wife, two sons, — John and Thomas, — aged respectively fourteen and twelve years, and three daughters, — Mary, Jane, and Rachel, — aged respectively nine, six, and three years. This little flock was his pride and delight, and I am sure there never lived a family happier in each other. They had, like all of us, their outside troubles, and at this time these came upon them with terrible force.

I have said that the Oxenford farm came to its present owner encumbered with his father's debts. These debts were very heavy, and for fourteen years Mr. Oxenford had exerted himself to pay them. He had reduced the amount very greatly; but, by the spring of 1773, the principal and interest of the aggregate claims against him amounted to very nearly the full value of the farm, and his creditors threatened that, as they saw no prospect of their payment, they would seize his property for their own protection, if their claims were not discharged in another year. This brought matters to a crisis; and, for a while, the future looked dark enough to the poor man. But Thomas Oxenford was a Christian man; and when his troubles were darkest, he sought the only arm that is all-powerful to save, and God heard him, as he hears the prayers of every soul that seeks him, and brought him through his troubles. Mr. Oxenford determined to sell his farm, and was fortunate enough to find a cash purchaser for it. With the money he received for it he paid the last debt due upon it, and then prepared to leave forever the home of his own and his children's childhood. It cost him a hard struggle to do this; for he loved the place dearly, both for its own sake and for the many happy hours he had passed there with his family. These ties, however, were broken, and the little family prepared to seek a new home.

After selling his farm, and paying the debts upon it, Mr. Oxenford found that he had a little less than seventy-five pounds left. This was a small sum for a man of family; but it was all he had to begin life afresh. To think of remaining in the older portion of the colony under such circumstances he felt to be madness, and he resolved to cross the mountains, and build up a home in the distant west. The hardy pioneers of that section had fairly settled the region lying along the lower waters of the Monongehela River, and, in several instances, had pushed their settlements as far west as the left bank of the Ohio. The country was new; but it had ceased to be the regular home of the savages, who had abandoned all parts of Virginia, and withdrawn to what is now the State of Ohio, and it was the place of all places which promised a rich reward to those who had the courage and fortitude to come out and conquer the wilderness. The savages, it is true, made frequent incursions into this section; but, as a general thing, they accomplished very little, and the whites had gained a foothold which every one felt was too firm to be forced back. Mr. Oxenford had heard rare stories of the beauty and fertility of the Ohio Valley, and had more than once contemplated a removal to it in case his difficulties came to the worst, and had only been prevented from putting this plan into execution by two very natural feelings — namely, a desire to remain in his old home, and a hope of conquering his ill fortune without subjecting his family to the hardships and inconvenience of such a removal; but now that there was no escape from the necessity of making a change, he determined to lose no time in setting out. The season was favorable, for it was the last of March, and by the first of April he hoped to begin his journey. He found able helpers in his wife and elder son. The brave woman was a true matron of our heroic days; and, though her heart bled at leaving forever the home in which her happiest years had been spent, she never murmured. Her only thought was to lighten the cares that had fallen upon her husband; and she proved, in this trying time, the value of a true wife and Christian woman. John, the eldest child, was delighted at the change. He had always wished to be an Indian hunter; and, as he could not be that just yet, he was glad to have an opportunity to see for himself something of pioneer life, boy-like, looking always upon the brightest side of the picture.

Well, there were many things to buy, and very little to buy them with. The seventy odd pounds left from the sale of the farm were increased to a hundred by the sale of such household goods as the family could not take with them; but even this sum proved barely sufficient to procure everything necessary for the change. There were provisions, ammunition, axes, guns, and a score of other different things to purchase, and it was necessary to keep a little money with them to buy such things as they might have need of on the journey, or during their first season in their new home. Of the stock on the farm, Mr. Oxenford kept only the cow, three of the horses, and a dog. The last was the children's pet, and he would not part with it.

Everything was in readiness at last, and, at sunrise on the first day of April, 1773, the adventurers turned their backs upon their old home, which they were never to see again; and, with a prayer to God that he would bless their undertaking, and carry them safely through the perils and trials before them, set their faces bravely toward the wilderness.

CHAPTER II.

THE EMIGRANTS.

My young reader may think it a very easy and very pleasant undertaking to journey from the Potomac to the Ohio, for he may have ridden over the route in the comfortable coaches of the Baltimore and Ohio Railroad, or the Pennsylvania Road; but he must remember that the time of which I am writing was long before the invention of steam, and even before the stage coaches had made their appearance west of the seaboard. At that day there were no broad, firm roads over the mountains, but in their place was merely the "trail," as it was called, left by the ill-fated expedition of General Braddock, and the military trail through Pennsylvania, by way of Bedford and Fort Ligonier to Fort Pitt, the site of the present city of Pittsburg. Very few persons took the latter route, as it was the longer of the two, and the majority followed Braddock's road, which, though the more difficult, was the more direct. It was this route that the Oxenfords selected; and, after leaving Loudon, they travelled slowly through the adjoining county to Winchester, in the Valley of Virginia, then a mere hamlet, and little better than a frontier post. Here Mr. Oxenford purchased a few articles of necessity, which he had not been able to procure at such short notice on the Potomac, and the journey was resumed in the direction of Fort Cumberland, in Maryland.

The three horses were made to carry the younger children and the household goods of the family. Two of them were provided with pack-saddles, upon which were loaded the articles to be transported; and the youngest children, who could not walk, were placed in hampers, one on each side of the horse, and the hampers were made fast to the horse's saddle. The pack-horses were led by John, the elder son. Thomas and Mary drove the cow along, Brindle having been secured against running away by means of a long rope which the little fellow held in one hand, and the father led the horse which carried the children, while the mother walked by his side. Thus they travelled towards their new home. They made slow progress at first; for the mother and children were unused to walking, and could not go far without resting. The weather was unusually fair, and it seemed as if Providence was smiling on their venture, and was making the way as pleasant for them as possible. Every evening towards sunset, having reached some suitable place for passing the night, the little band would halt, and build a roaring fire, and the mother, with the assistance of the others, would prepare supper, which was often made palatable by a dish of game which the father or John would secure during the day. Supper over, the family Bible was brought out, and, by the light of the fire, Thomas Oxenford would read to the little band gathered around him those blessed words which can give strength to the weak and courage to the faint-hearted, and which can cheer the heart when everything human has failed. Indeed, I think God's Holy Word has never been so carefully and constantly read by any persons as by those who "planted the wilderness" in the early days of which I am writing. It was not because it was the only book they had that they studied its pages so faithfully. They had a higher, a more powerful motive. They felt as we, their children, rarely feel, the power of the Lord Jehovah, and their need of his aid. They had gone out trusting in him, and they had every day proof that without him they could do nothing. We, with our comforts and "modern improvements," are too apt to forget, and still more apt to fail to acknowledge, this dependence. But our forefathers were wiser than we. Having finished the chapter, Mr. Oxenford would ask God's blessing on their undertaking, and his guidance on their lonely way, and then the dim forest would ring with the strains of some sweet old hymn — words they could not sing without tears; for they carried them back to their old home, which they would see no more forever. Then they went to rest — the children wrapped in their blankets, and laid on beds of forest leaves, and the older members of the family finding their beds on the ground. One member was always awake, to keep up the fire, which was a safeguard against wild beasts, and to see that no danger befell the sleepers. This duty was generally performed by the parents and the elder son. John, being unused to vigils such as these, was given what the sailors call the "dog watch," or, in other words, he stood guard from the family bed-time till ten o'clock. Then his mother relieved him, and his father relieved her at two o'clock, giving the wife and son the longest times for sleep. At sunrise, the next day, the camp was astir, and the day was opened, as the previous one had closed, with prayer and praise. Then followed breakfast, after which the journey was resumed.

In due time, Fort Cumberland, where now stands the thriving city of Cumberland, in Maryland, was reached and passed, and in a few days our emigrants had crossed the Monongehela, near its junction with the Youghiogeny. They were now fairly over the Allegheny Mountains, and were very near the scene of Braddock's defeat in Western Pennsylvania. This region was beginning to attract settlers; but Mr. Oxenford was desirous of going farther west; so, leaving Braddock's trail, at the point where he crossed the Monongehela, he journeyed towards the Ohio, which he reached, a few days later, at a point about twenty-five miles below the site of the present city of Wheeling, the capital of the State of West Virginia.

It so happened that he came in sight of the Ohio near the mouth of Fish Creek. Pleased with the beauty of the country, and detecting, at a glance, — for he was a thorough farmer, — the good qualities of the soil, he determined to make this section his home. He could not have chosen a better time for his first view of the country. It was the middle of April, and the spring was far advanced. The grass was grown, and it covered the whole earth with a robe of the richest green — a hue which the shade of the hills that shut in the valley seemed to deepen. The dogwood blossoms were out, and the buttercups and wild violets were sparkling all through the grass. The breeze which swept down from the hills was balmy and sweet, and the very breath of it seemed to give new life to our emigrants. They paused involuntarily on a little knoll commanding a distant view of the river and creek, and simultaneously they exclaimed that they had found their home. It had been twenty days since they had left their old home in Loudon, and now they had reached the end of their wanderings.

Deeming it imprudent to locate himself so near the river, as the sight of his dwelling, when built, might prove a constant temptation to the Indians on the opposite side of the Ohio, Mr.

Oxenford determined to go a mile or so farther up the creek; and, following the shore, they reached, by nightfall, a spot about six miles from the river, where they determined to locate themselves. It was too late, however, to do anything that night, and the family went to rest early, determined to rise the next morning with the lark, and lay the foundation of their future home.

CHAPTER III.

BUILDING AND CLEARING.

WORN out by the long journey and the fatigue of the previous day, Mr. Oxenford, to whom was assigned the morning watch, fell asleep by the fire towards daybreak. He was aroused by some one placing a hand on his shoulder. Starting up in alarm, he seized his gun, and looked about him. There was no one near but John, who was laughing at his father's alarm. The sun was shining brightly, but the other members of the family were still sleeping.

"Why, father," said John, laughing, "you look as though you expected to see an Indian."

"To tell the truth, I did," said Mr. Oxenford, laying down his gun with an air of relief. "I deserved to be surprised for sleeping on my post. It is the first time, however, and it shall be the last. But what are you so happy about?"

"O, father," cried the boy, rubbing his hands, gleefully," the creek is full of fish—full of fish."

"We shall have to let the fish alone for a while, my boy," said Mr. Oxenford. "After we get our house started, we can turn our attention to the fish. Now let us wake your mother and the children, and have breakfast."

Mrs. Oxenford and her children were soon awakened, and in less than an hour they were all seated at breakfast, having washed their faces in the clear waters of the creek, and given thanks to the Creator for his goodness to them. Breakfast over, the next thing was to prepare for building a dwelling.

The family had encamped, on the previous night, upon a slight hill, at a distance of a few hundred yards from the creek, and sloping down to it; and Mr. Oxenford decided, after a brief survey, to make their camping-ground the site of their home. There was no time to be lost about it, and, taking his axe, the settler commenced to clear the summit of the hill. John was eager to assist in this work, and as there were two axes at hand, his father gave him one, and the brave boy fell to work with a will. He was well grown for his age, and was as strong as a young bullock. His sturdy blows told well on the trees, and he managed his work so well that he bade fair to rival his father in the task before them. Two days were passed in this manner, and on the morning of the third day, Mr. Oxenford said they had cut timber enough, and must now proceed to prepare the logs for building. This was another two days' task, and on the morning of the fifth day they had piled their logs ready for use, and had split boards or slabs enough from the larger trees to form the roof and floor of their new dwelling. Then came the clearing up of the ground, which occupied another day; and the sixth day, which happened to be Saturday, was passed in boring the logs with an auger, wherever it was necessary to do so, and making wooden pins to fasten the work together, for there were no nails within reach of the settlers. Sunday was a day of rest; and, in the absence of a church, the pious father called his family around him, and, after a prayer, a hymn, and a chapter from the Bible, spoke to them upon such subjects as he deemed most appropriate to the day and to their situation.

Monday morning they were all up bright and early. The ground was swept free from the leaves which had fallen upon it, and the father and mother and the two boys commenced to build the house, while Mary, the eldest daughter, looked after her little sisters. They worked bravely, and by nightfall they had done fully half the work. By a dexterous use of his saw and hatchet, Mr. Oxenford made the logs and the slab-floor fit admirably; and Mrs. Oxenford and the boys assisted him in arranging them, and fastening the pins in their places. There was an abundance of stones, of all sizes, along the shore of the creek, and these furnished the means of constructing a hearth and a chimney, while the mud, which soon hardened, formed a very handy mortar for holding the stones together, and filling up the crevices between the logs. By the afternoon of the third day, Wednesday, the roof was on, and the house almost ready for occupancy.

My readers must not imagine that this was a very roomy mansion, or that the task of building it was a very light one. It took nearly a fortnight to clear the ground, and build the house, which was nothing more than a plain log cabin, such as some of you may have seen in the mountains, or in the far south, on the plantations. It had but two rooms on the ground floor, and a loft above, which was reached by means of a rough ladder, which the boys made. There was one window in the side looking from the creek; but as such a thing as window glass was not to be had, the opening was closed by means of a stout slab shutter, or blind. This window could be used for the purpose of giving light only in warm weather, and during a rain, or the cold season, it would have to remain closed. The floor was made of rough slabs, partially planed down,—for Mr. Oxenford had been thoughtful enough to bring with him a small stock of carpenter's tools,—and the roof was constructed of heavy clapboards, which he had split from the trees, and the underside of which he lined with a kind of thatching of pine boughs and dry grass. To be sure, it was not such a dwelling as they had left behind, beyond the mountains; but it was a shelter, and that was a great thing to persons who had been living in the open air for more than a month. The walls were rough, and the long streaks of mud which filled the crevices between the logs looked bad enough; but, on the whole, the cabin presented a tolerably fair appearance, and, more than this, it was the work of their own hands, and they were very well satisfied with it. Some weeks afterwards the appearance of the walls was improved by nailing, with wooden pins, a row of wooden strips along the "chinks" of mud. This was also an additional comfort, as it made the cabin much warmer. The door, which was also made of slabs, was swung on a wooden hinge, and fastened by day with a latch, and at night by means of a heavy bar cross it inside.

Mrs. Oxenford had been careful to bring with her the ticking of her beds, and while the cabin was building, she had gathered leaves and dry grass, which she had carefully spread and dried again in the sun; and by the time the cabin was finished, she had collected and dried enough to make beds for all the family. She and the younger boy filled the tickings, and carried them into the cabin, where they were laid on the floor, and on Saturday night the little family had the satisfaction of sleeping in their new home.

The next Monday, the house being finished, Mr. Oxenford set about clearing up a patch of land, in order to plant the seed-corn he had brought with him. It was early in May, and he was in good season for his planting. He had brought with him a supply of corn-meal, which he hoped would last, by careful economy, until the first crop should be grown. He determined to locate his cornfield in the bottom land, bordering on the creek, rightly judging that this low land was richer than that on the hills. He selected a piece about six acres in extent, — a very respectable plantation for a pioneer, — and commenced to clear it up. Fortunately, there were very few trees on this part of the land. It was covered mostly with a low undergrowth of weeds and pawpaw bushes, which did not require so much exertion as the cutting down of trees. The work to be done consisted principally of what the farmers call "grubbing;" and even the children could assist in this, so that in another week the land was ready for planting.

The trouble now was to make a plough; but John, who was very much of a mechanical genius, soon remedied this by taking his father's tools, and making a very good substitute for an iron tiller of the soil. To be sure the plough had a wooden point; but then the boy had chosen a piece of tough maple, and had done his work so well that there was no doubt that the plough would answer for one season, at least. The ground was soft, and almost black with fertility, and would only require to be broken a little; and so, though it was slow work, John's plough answered the purpose admirably. The construction of a harrow was an easier task; and this the boy performed while his father was ploughing the land. He fastened the triangular frame of the harrow with wooden pegs, and made the teeth of stout oaken pins, which he drove in the auger holes he had bored in the frame. The harrow answered as well as the plough, and by the twentieth of May the corn was planted. The next thing in order was to plant the potatoes which they had brought out. An acre of land adjoining the cornfield was laid off, and, thanks to John's plough and harrow, this was soon planted.

Meanwhile, John had worked hard. He had made his mother a table, which consisted of a large slab of wood, supported on four sticks, two at each end, stuck in as many auger holes. This answered for their meals, and for the household work. They had brought out their cooking utensils and some tin ware with them, and were well supplied with these articles. John made stools, which were miniature copies of the table, and a row of shelves, which he put up with creditable neatness. He drove a row of pegs along the wall, to answer the place of a clothes-press, and helped his father to make a rough bedstead for each of their three beds. These things were done during such moments as they could spare from other work, and by the beginning of the summer they had provided almost everything that was absolutely necessary to their comfort. To be sure, these things were very rough, but they answered their purpose, and that was all that was required of them.

By this time a little patch had been laid off for a garden, and planted with such garden seed as they had brought with them. Their corn-meal continued to hold out, and the fish in the creek proved to be of the finest kind, such as "jack," bass, and pike, with an abundance of fresh-water herrings and suckers. The boys attended to this duty, and rarely a day passed that they did not bring in a fine mess with their little seine.

The cow, the horses, and the pigs — for I had forgotten to mention that the family had brought with them a pair of fine swine for the purpose of raising their pork — were kept up, the pigs in a pen, and the other animals tied to trees. The land afforded the best possible grazing, and to little Thomas, who was too young to do much of the work allotted to the rest, was given the task of seeing that the animals were fed and watered, and prevented from running off.

John, as I have said, was a good-sized boy. He could handle the plough, the carpenter's tools, and the rifle, almost as well as his father; and, as I have shown, he was of the greatest assistance to his parents. His disposition was lively and cheerful, and no matter how hard was his work, he was never cast down. Everything seemed bright and cheering to him.

He said he meant to persevere, and that after a while the country would be settled, and he would make a fortune, and build a fine house where they had located their cabin — a resolution which he literally carried out fifty years later.

One morning, soon after their arrival at Fish Creek, Mrs. Oxenford saw John come up to the cabin quickly, take his gun and go off silently and rapidly. His father's orders against wasting ammunition were very strict, and as she saw the eager look on the boy's face, she felt a momentary alarm, for fear there was danger from the Indians. She called after John to come back; but he was too far to hear her, and she stood in the cabin door, watching him as he disappeared into the woods, and anxiously waiting to learn what would follow. In a few minutes she heard the report of his rifle, followed by a loud hurrah, in a tone so gleeful that it dispelled her fear at once; and the next instant John dashed out of the woods, dragging something after him, and, coming towards his mother at full speed, laid in triumph at her feet an immense wild turkey.

"I killed him myself, mother," said the boy, proudly. "Isn't he a fine fellow? And look, what a splendid shot; I aimed for his eye, and I've hit him fair in the head."

It was, indeed, a "fine fellow," and the boy had a right to be proud. He had seen the turkey in the woods, and had determined on securing it. It was their first game since their arrival, and it lasted them for nearly three days. After this, they had an abundance of game, consisting of wild turkeys, squirrels, and, once or twice, a deer. The country was full of such provisions, and Mr. Oxenford said, after he had finished clearing up his place, he would set to work to lay in a supply of venison.

Thus the weeks passed away. Every one worked, — for there was no room for idlers in such a community, — and by the middle of August they had built and furnished their cabin, and a stable, which they thatched with pine boughs, for the horses and the cow, and which

THE YOUNG HUNTER'S FIRST WILD TURKEY. Page 36.

they located but a few yards from the house. Adjoining the stable they built a crib, in which to stow away their corn for the winter, after it was harvested, and had commenced to form a wood-pile near the cabin, which should constitute their stock of fuel for the winter.

CHAPTER IV.

THE SETTLEMENT.

LITTLE Thomas had taken the cattle out to graze, one morning, and half an hour after his departure he came running back at full speed.

"Father, father," he shouted, "come see the big cow that's down at the creek. Come quick!"

Mr. Oxenford took down his rifle from the bracket on the wall, and, following the little fellow, who was eager to act as guide, hastened down to the creek. As he came in sight of it, he saw a large buffalo drinking at the water's edge. The animal was utterly unconscious of the presence of a human being, and was drinking leisurely. Mr. Oxenford had suspected the nature of the stranger as soon as his son had called it a cow, and he was eager to secure the prize. Bidding Thomas conceal himself behind a tree, and keep very still, he crept cautiously towards the animal, until he came within easy range of it. Then, taking his position where he could see without being seen by the beast, he prepared to take advantage of its movements. The buffalo, however, seemed in no hurry; for when he had finished drinking, he walked into the creek a little way, and stood with the water reaching to his keees, as if to cool his legs and hoofs, for the day was warm. Mr. Oxenford feared he would continue his course, swim the creek, and thus escape him; but this fear was soon dispelled, for the animal turned quietly, and came back to the shore. Pausing there for a moment, he lowered his head to cross the fresh grass that grew close to the water. Now was the hunter's opportunity, and, aiming his rifle carefully, Mr. Oxenford fired. The ball struck the buffalo just back of the ear, and the huge animal fell over on his side, struggling feebly, and trying to rise.

The next moment Mr. Oxenford had drawn his hunting-knife across its throat, making a deep gash from ear to ear, from which the blood gushed in a perfect stream. The buffalo ceased his struggles, and, with a spasmodic quiver, fell back dead. He was a huge animal, and would have been worth a small fortune to a butcher in these modern days of high prices; and Mr. Oxenford resolved that he would get the full value of the brute.

Going back to the cabin, he removed his outer garments, that he might not soil them, and took the largest tin pail, and the hatchet, which he meant to use in place of a cleaver, and, calling John to help him, went back to the spot where he had left the buffalo. The father and son were novices in the task before them; but they went at it with a determination that made up for their lack of practice, and by sunset they had stripped the animal of his hide, and had cut off all the meat that they could use for the present, and a large quantity that they designed for curing. The hide and horns were carefully washed and put away, and the remains of the animal were cast into the creek, where they either sank from sight or floated away on the current. They had a fine breakfast and dinner the next day on "Tom's cow," as they called it; and what could not be kept for use next day — and this was fully nine tenths of the meat — was suspended from a young sapling over a smoke made by a quantity of green hickory chips being heaped on a slow fire. This process of curing was very simple and easily performed, and by means of it they were able to preserve their meat for use whenever they needed it. In this same way they cured much venison during the year.

It lacked but four weeks until the harvesting season, when a trouble, which had not been foreseen, occurred.

"Thomas," said Mrs. Oxenford, one day, her face wearing a graver look than it had ever worn, "what shall we do for bread? Our corn-meal is gone, and we can get no more until the harvest."

"We'll have to live on meat until then, old lady," said her husband, cheerily. "W've got a plenty of that, I am glad to know, and there's no danger of our starving."

Those of my readers who have never been compelled to go without bread can hardly tell what it is to be deprived of it. The Oxenfords were not slow in finding out that it was indeed the "staff of life." After living on meat alone for several days, it became sickening and distasteful to them, and at the end of a week they became sickly. Their stomachs were always uncomfortable; that is, they had a feeling of emptiness, and were always tormented by a sensation of hunger. John, who always tried to make the best of their troubles, called the lean breast of the wild turkey bread, and the other flesh, such as venison and dried beef, meat; but though they tried to be satisfied with the substitute, none of them could fully withstand the consequences of the absence of the real bread. How anxiously they watched the cornfield and the little garden for the first roasting ears and vegetables! and what a jubilee they had when John brought in the first ear of young corn, and his father said they would now have roasting ears and boiled corn until the harvest came! This was an improvement on their previous situation, and was soon followed by the ripening of the vegetables in the garden. Every one began to grow strong and vigorous again.

As the harvest drew near, a new difficulty presented itself to the family. They would have plenty of corn; but how were they to convert it into meal? This question was soon settled by Mrs. Oxenford, who suggested a plan which afterwards was put into execution. Taking one of the tin pails, Mr. Oxenford, at his wife's suggestion, carefully removed the bottom, and then, cutting the side of the remainder, he laid the sheet of tin out flat on a board, and by means of a punch cut a number of holes in the sheet. In this way he made a sort of rude grater, and bending it to a semicircular form, he nailed it to a block of wood with bits of nails made from the wire which had formed the handle of the pail. After the harvest was gathered in, this primitive mill was tried, and it was found to answer tolerably well. The corn was taken in the ear, and rubbed over the rough side of the grater, and was thus grated to a fineness sufficient for the manufacture of johnny-cakes and coarse pones, or pieces of corn-bread worked and shaped with the hands. The meal made by the use of this grater was not as fine as that they had brought with them from the old colony; but still it was meal, and gave them bread.

The harvest was gathered in in due time, and it was bountiful, proving far more than would be sufficient for the family until the next season. The corn was husked and piled up in the "crib," which barely held it, and the potatoes were stowed away, when gathered, in a cellar which was dug near the house. The fodder was stacked close by the stable, and this, with the corn-husks, gave the assurance of a plentiful supply of provender for the cattle, and there remained nothing but to prepare the wood-pile for the winter; and by the time the cold weather had fairly set in, this, too, was accomplished. So, one bright autumn morning, when the harvest was in, and everything was in readiness for the long winter which was coming, Mr. Oxenford declared they would devote one day to rest from all labor, and make it the occasion for returning thanks to the Almighty for the blessings he had showered upon them. This was done, and it was the first "Thanksgiving Day" observed on the banks of the Ohio. They had everything to be thankful for. The Lord's hand had led them to one of the most desirable portions of the west, and had kept them safely ever since. There had been no sickness in their midst, and they had been called upon to endure only the ordinary hardships of the settler's life. They had been successful in all their undertakings, and were now in a condition to look forward to the winter without dreading it.

Thomas Oxenford was especially grateful. At the beginning of the spring he was without a home for his family, and the owner of but a little over seventy pounds sterling. Now he had made a home for his little flock, and was the proprietor of four hundred acres of the land surrounding his cabin, which was the freehold given by the laws of the colony to every settler who should build a house and raise a crop of grain on any unoccupied land west of the Allegheny Mountains. Besides this, his act of settlement gave him a pre-emption right to one thousand acres more of the adjoining land; and all that remained for him to do was to fix upon the boundaries of his land, so as to avoid difficulties with the settlers who might follow him. It was true that this land had yet to be cleared up and cultivated, and that this involved much toil and hardship for his family; but still they had a home, and the certainty of making a livelihood, however plain and humble it might be.

The "Thanksgiving Day" was drawing to

a close, and the little family were gathered around their evening meal, — for this was always served before dark in those days, — when they were startled by a loud "halloo" from without. It had been so long since they had heard any human voices but their own, that they started to their feet in alarm, and rushed to the door. Their astonishment was complete when they saw, standing a few yards from them, a party of men, women, and children and seven or eight horses, loaded with goods of various kinds. The sight was so novel and unexpected that both parties stared at each other for some moments in silence. At last Mr. Oxenford went forward, and, greeting the new comers cordially, — for he was glad to see some of his own species besides his family after so long an absence from them, — asked, —

"Well, my friends, what are you doing here?"

"We came here to settle, stranger," said one of the men; "but it seems you've got ahead of us."

"There's land enough for all of us, and many more," said Mr. Oxenford, laughing, in spite of himself, at the disappointment evinced by the man. "You shall all stay here with us to-night, and to-morrow we'll see what we can do."

The new comers were emigrants from the upper portion of Maryland and Virginia, and consisted of four families, numbering in all about twenty-six people, of whom ten were men and half-grown boys. The heads of these families were people in the prime of life, — the very best material for pioneers, — and there were no very young children in the party. They had met by accident while crossing the mountains, and had concluded to cast their lot together, rather than separate, thinking rightly that they could accomplish more by united than by independent exertions. They had supposed they were the first who had penetrated this region, until they saw the clearing and cabin of Mr. Oxenford, and were astonished to find such deep traces of civilization where they expected to see nothing but the wilderness, and they were profuse in their praise of the settlers' industry and energy. They brought with them an abundance of provisions, and among other things had a large quantity of salt, which they agreed to share with the Oxenfords for a supply of their corn.

The women and youngest children were made comfortable in the cabin during the night, and the male portion of the little community encamped in the yard, for the weather was still sufficiently mild and favorable for them to do so. The new comers had just left the older colonies, and they had an abundance of news to communicate. The troubles with the mother country were then agitating the new world, and the emigrants were loud in their denunciation of the course pursued by Great Britain. One family had come from the neighborhood in which the Oxenfords had lived, and were able to tell them about their friends east of the mountains. The night was far spent when they sought their beds, and each felt grateful to Providence for having drawn them together.

The next morning they were up early, and, breakfast over, the heads of the different families assembled with Mr. Oxenford to consult as to their future movements. It was agreed that it was impossible for any one to cultivate all the land to which he was entitled, and that it would be better for them to unite in clearing up a number of acres, and cultivate that in common until they were fairly settled. They could lay off their lands, and after they had thoroughly arranged their settlement they could divide the land and cultivate it separately. This arrangement would be in force for about one or two years, and should their settlement be increased in the mean while by the addition of other emigrants, they could pursue a similar plan towards them. Acting upon this conclusion, they at once proceeded to lay off their lands; and as they were all practical farmers, they succeeded in forming a proximate idea of the quantity of land necessary to make up four hundred acres to each man. They wisely determined that their farms should have a narrow frontage on the creek, which would bring them nearer together, and that their length should be the longer line of boundary. This mode of arrangement made the Oxenford farm the centre of the little settlement, and it was determined to cultivate the creek line first. This would enable them to join their fields to that commenced by Mr. Oxenford, and they could all cultivate them in common. The sites chosen for their cabins were all on the ridge upon which the original settlers had built theirs, and were located at such easy distances that the farthest on the right and left hand — the original cabin being the centre — was only half a mile from the Oxenfords. The boundaries of the different "claims," as they were called, were marked by cutting the trees in a straight line for a distance of half a mile back from the creek.

When these preliminaries were arranged,

the settlers prepared to clear up their land for building. Instead of working separately at this, they decided to unite. Lots were then drawn to determine whose house should be built first, and, having settled this matter, all turned in with a will, and commenced the building. Mr. Oxenford and John lent a willing assistance in this work, and this made a force of twelve workers. After the trees were felled, and the logs prepared, it was found that this force was too much for one cabin, and it was divided into parties of six each, and in this way two cabins were put up at the same time. In a week all the cabins were finished, and the little settlement had begun to assume a thriving and spirited appearance. The next week was given to building the stables and such out-houses as were necessary. The buildings were all situated on the brow of the ridge that lay back at a distance of several hundred yards from the creek, and almost sixty yards from the woods. They were all in sight of each other, and as the new emigrants proved pleasant and industrious people, Mr. Oxenford was glad that his family would now have something to relieve the loneliness that all of them were beginning to feel.

Later in the season other families arrived at the settlement, and most of these went over to the south side of Fish Creek, where they built their dwellings and cleared their land, so that by the time the winter had fairly set in, the settlement had increased to ten families, or, in all, to nearly sixty persons.

The Oxenfords had, during this time, done much to improve their condition. They had made themselves comfortable by the addition of a considerable amount of home-made furniture, which I am inclined to think my young readers would consider very uncomfortable. After the harvest they had emptied their beds of their fillings of leaves and grass, and had replaced them with the soft, dry husks of the corn. This made an excellent bed, and was a great improvement upon the leaves.

At last the cold weather set in. The winter is long and bleak in this portion of the Ohio Valley, and it was fortunate that the settlers had succeeded in making their preparations to withstand it. The wood-piles now became more valuable in the eyes of their owners than they had ever supposed they would be. Having their fuel cut and piled at their doors, they were saved the trouble of cutting and hauling it in the deep snows.

The first snow was a treat to the younger members of the community, for, though they were pioneers, they were still boys, and were as fond of sport as any of those of the present day. John Oxenford was a great authority among them, though several of them were older than he, for his mechanical skill and ingenuity were greater than those of his fellows; and when the snow came, he proposed that they should make sledges at once, so that they might have as much sport at coasting as they had enjoyed in their old homes. The proposal was caught up eagerly, and in spite of the cold and the blinding flakes, the boys started out, hatchet in hand, to cut hickory saplings for runners, and by nightfall they made full half a dozen sledges. They were very rough, but they were strong, and the hickory runners were scraped as smooth as glass. I think the young people of to-day, with their handsome "coasters," with brightly-painted sides, cushioned seats, and steel runners, would consider these frontier sledges but a sorry show; but I doubt that they derive any more enjoyment from their costly toys than did these sturdy little pioneers with their home-made substitutes. The next day the snow ceased falling, and the clouds cleared off, and with a shout the boys started for the hill-side, where they were soon dashing down the slope at a speed which made their mothers — who watched them from the cabin doors — tremble for their limbs; but nobody was hurt. The boys had their fun. The sledges were stout, and well made, and there were no broken bones to mend. A few bruises were gotten by some, but they were nothing. And then, such fun as the youngsters had with their snow-balls! It was a real treat to see them.

"Now, fellows," said John Oxenford, when the snow was gone, "we must get our traps ready for the next snow-fall. There'll be lots of rabbits about, and they'll come in very handy, father says."

So it was arranged; and when the ground was white again with the soft flakes, the traps were set. The first day passed away without success. Big Dan Whittaker, the son of one of the settlers, was the first to catch a rabbit, and the boys were wild with delight. There was no envy of Dan's success among the little fellows. Boys are slow to grudge each other a triumph fairly won. Every one liked Dan, for, awkward and overgrown as he was, he was the very impersonation of generosity and good nature. He was John Oxenford's sworn friend, and the two were inseparable. They were like David and Jonathan, and I am sure Dan would have risked his life, willingly, to do John a service, and John was equally as devoted. If one made a paw-paw whistle, or found a lot of ripe nuts, he was sure to make a similar provision for the other; and wherever you saw one, you might be sure the other was close at hand.

During the winter, the supply of salt was found to be running low, and it became necessary to send to the settlement at Wheeling, about twenty-five miles higher up the Ohio River, for more. Mr. Oxenford and Mr. Brady were chosen to go after it, and they set out about the middle of January, taking advantage of a temporary absence of snow. They reached the little hamlet of Wheeling, which had been settled a few years before, about dark on the day after their departure from Fish Creek. They found the place full of rumors of trouble with the Indians. It was said that the governor of the colony, Lord Dunmore, was bent upon destroying the savages as soon as the weather should be favorable enough for the movement of the troops. This news filled Mr. Oxenford with grave uneasiness, and he sought an interview with the officer in command of Fort Fincastle, which was the name given to the work — afterwards known as Fort Henry — that had been erected for the defence of the village. He explained to the commandant the exposed situation of the settlement on Fish Creek, and asked his advice as to the best course to be pursued by himself and his neighbors.

Colonel Shepherd, the commandant of the fort, informed him that the rumors he had heard were, unfortunately, true, and that there was no doubt that the Indians would cause considerable trouble on the frontier in the spring, if, indeed, they did not do so before the close of the winter. He advised Mr. Oxenford to urge upon his neighbors the propriety of establishing some means of defence, such as the building of a fort or stockade, and as a means of assisting him in this undertaking, the colonel carried him over the work under his command, and gave him some general ideas upon the subject. The colonel was an old soldier, and had seen service in the French wars, and his opinions were of value to the settlers, who determined that they would spare no effort to urge them upon their neighbors.

The salt was obtained at a reasonable sum, and the next day the two settlers returned to Fish Creek, which they reached about nightfall.

CHAPTER V.

THE FORT.

THE morning after the return of the two settlers from Wheeling, a meeting of all the adult males in the little settlement was held at Mr. Oxenford's cabin, and that gentleman revealed to his neighbors the information he had received from Colonel Shepherd. Since their arrival at Fish Creek they had seen no one from the other settlements, and were in total ignorance of the condition of affairs in the rest of the country. They had been unmolested by the Indians, not one of whom had appeared at the settlement, and could hardly believe the truth of Colonel Shepherd's statement, that the savages were becoming very troublesome on the border. Still, they agreed that it would be most prudent to take some measure of a defensive nature, and it was finally determined to erect a fort for the protection of their families. This was an undertaking which would require some little time, and it was decided to commence it at once. The weather was clear and cold, and the ground was free from snow, so that, by exerting themselves, they might at least get through with a portion of the work before the next fall of snow; and as Mr. Oxenford and Mr. Brady had seen the fort at Wheeling, they were appointed to superintend the construction of the fortification. These deliberations occupied about two hours of the morning, and as soon as they were ended, the work was begun.

The first thing was to lay off the ground on which the fort was to be built. The object being to establish a place of refuge in times of danger, the location would have to be convenient to all parts of the settlement, and therefore it was decided to erect the work as nearly in the centre of the little hamlet as possible. This would make it convenient to the settlers south of the creek, as well as to those north of the stream. The site chosen was about fifty yards west of the Oxenfords' cabin, and about seventy yards from the woods. It was the highest point of the settlement, and commanded a view of the entire neighborhood. It was but a few yards from the spring which supplied the settlers with water, and was believed to be the best defensive position that could be selected. The younger boys were set to clearing off the ground, and the men and older boys at once went into the woods to cut the logs necessary for the fort. An entire week was spent in cutting and hauling the logs, during which time there was a slight flurry of snow, but not enough to suspend the efforts of the workmen. The next week the ground was staked off, and the building was begun in earnest.

If my readers are under the impression that the settlers at Fish Creek were about to attempt the construction of such a "fort" as those of us who saw anything of our late war, or who have seen the massive works which protect our sea-coast, are familiar with, they are very much mistaken. A frontier fort was merely a stockade; and as the savages had no weapons but rifles, this was found amply sufficient for the defence of the pioneers.

The fort at Fish Creek was built upon the plan generally adopted along the border. It was a square in shape, with a block-house at each corner. A row of five cabins was built on the west side, and a similar row on the east side; and as it was probable that the settlement might be increased, or that settlers in the neighborhood might seek shelter in the fort, it was decided to erect a row of cabins on the north side, while the south side was fitted up as a row of stables for the stock. The outer walls of these buildings were constructed of heavy logs, in the same manner that the dwellings in the settlement were built, except that the chinks, after being filled up with mud, were covered with stout oaken boards, in order to make them bullet-proof. The walls were twelve feet high on the exterior, and the roofs sloped inward. The floors of the cabins were made of slabs, and the chimneys of rocks and mud. At each corner of the square formed by the rows of cabins, a strong tower, or block-house, was built of the heaviest logs. These block-houses were two stories in height, and projected about three feet beyond the outer walls of the cabins. The second story was eighteen inches larger in length and width than the first story, and that part of the floor which extended over the lower wall was pierced for firing through it, in order to prevent the enemy from getting close under the sides of the fort, and thus avoiding the fire of the garrison. The sides of the block-houses and the outer walls of the cabins were pierced with loop-holes at the proper height, and at a distance of five feet apart in the cabins, and two feet in the block-houses. On the south side, and just opposite the spring, the gate was placed. It was made of heavy slabs, firmly pinned together, and was secured in its place by stout bars of wood. The entrance was large enough to allow the passage with ease of three horses abreast, and the gate was double, or "folding." The stables were also loop-holed, and every precaution taken to enable a heavy fire to be directed against any party that should try to break in the gate. In the centre of the enclosure thus made, a large log building, which was properly a double cabin, was erected. This was intended to serve as a storehouse, and was also made bullet-proof and loop-holed, so that it might serve as a kind of citadel to the garrison, in case the enemy should succeed in overcoming the outer defences. The cabins were separated from each other by partitions of logs, so that each family should have its own house, and maintain its separate establishment. After the fort was completed, it was decided to dig a well in the enclosure, so that the garrison, during a siege, might not be deprived of water; and this was done in the spring, after the frost had gone out of the ground.

It took seven weeks of hard labor to build the fort, but it was finished by the second week in March, 1774. The work was done faithfully, for the settlers said they meant to make their fort impregnable to any attack from the savages, as the work was worth doing well, if it was worth doing at all. The whole fort covered an area about one hundred and five feet square, and it was as strong as the skill of the builders could make it. Their efforts had been stimulated by a warning which had been sent them from Fort Fincastle, at Wheeling, that matters were growing worse every day, and that they had better be on the watch for a visit from the Indians at any moment. They were not disturbed, however, and the fort was ready at last. The next week was passed in providing it with stores of various kinds. A large wood-pile was formed in the yard, to provide fuel during a siege, and each member of the little community contributed a portion of his provisions and ammunition, so that there should be a supply in the storehouse capable of sustaining the settlers, who should take refuge in the fort, for at least a week. These things were placed in the storehouse, and it was understood that no one was to touch them without the consent of the person who should be placed in charge of the fort. There were more cabins than were needed for the use of the settlers then present, and, in order to prevent confusion when it should be necessary to occupy the fort, the cabins were assigned to the various families by drawing lots for them.

The last thing done was the election of a commanding officer for the fort, and the choice fell upon Mr. Oxenford, who was thenceforth styled "Captain." It was decided that the captain should abandon his former dwelling, and take up his quarters in the fort, as it was necessary that some one should occupy the work, and thus have it prepared for any surprise on the part of the savages; and it was not practicable that the whole community should dwell in it all the time. In consideration of this, Captain Oxenford was allowed to occupy one of the block-houses, and a cabin adjoining it, which he was permitted to fit up with the greatest degree of comfort consistent with the defensive nature of the building. The settlers then pledged their honor to render to their commander the strictest obedience, and it was agreed that all cases of disobedience in time of actual war with the savages should be punished by a fine of twenty bushels of corn, to be added to the supplies in the storehouse, and in times of peace with the savages the fine was to be ten bushels of corn. During hostilities the captain's will was to be the law of the settlement, from which there was to be no appeal; but in times of peace, an appeal might be had from him to a jury of four settlers, two to be selected by him, and two by the person making the appeal.

After his selection for the command of the fort, Captain Oxenford prepared to remove his family to their new home. He and John, with the assistance of Dan Whittaker and another neighbor, transferred the flooring and the greater part of the work on his cabin to the fort, and in a few days they had made the block-house and cabin as snug as they were able. Then the family moved in, and took possession. They had more room by this arrangement than they had formerly, as the block-house was two stories high. They fastened pieces of plank over the loop-holes to keep out the cold and wind, arranging the coverings so that they could be removed at a moment's notice. They continued to use their old stable and other out-houses. The cabin they had occupied as a dwelling was simply closed up. Captain Oxenford said it had better remain there, as it might be useful at some time.

By the time all these things were arranged the spring had fairly opened, and the settlers commenced to prepare for planting their corn and potatoes, and making their gardens. Two or three hunters arrived at the settlement about this time, and were assigned one of the cabins in the fort, upon the condition that they should do their part towards providing the fort with a supply of meat. They did nothing towards tilling the land, as they were constantly roaming the woods; but they paid for their living by supplying the various families with game.

They were a wild, rough set, but generous and kind-hearted. They were old Indian-fighters, too; and, as the country was on the eve of a war with the savages, the settlers were glad to have these men with them, as their experience in border warfare would, no doubt, be useful to them.

As I have said, those who had settled on the north shore of the creek cultivated their land in common, and divided the corn crop and the fodder. This proved an excellent plan, as it enabled them to work a large amount of land, and, as the harvest showed, to make a very heavy crop. Every one worked hard this spring, for all felt that, as the Indians might interfere with them the next season, it was necessary to raise as much corn as possible.

One morning John was sent from the "bottom," where all hands were at work, to get something which his father had left in the loft of his old cabin. He hurried to the building, ascended to the loft, and soon found the article he had been sent for. As he was about to descend, he heard the sound of a heavy footfall in the room below. He called to know what was wanted; but as no one answered, he went to the opening in the floor through which he had ascended to the loft, and looked down. To his surprise and alarm, he saw a large black bear, sitting on its haunches, and gazing cunningly towards the loft. The animal had heard the boy when he called out, and had prepared himself to await his descent. He was a powerful-looking monster; and as he saw the boy at the opening in the floor, he uttered a low growl, and licked his huge jaws with his bright-red tongue, in a manner that made John's blood run cold.

John Oxenford was a brave boy, and, for one of his age, was possessed of a remarkable degree of coolness and self-possession. Though he was greatly alarmed at the imminence of his danger, his courage did not forsake him. He knew it was vain to hope for relief at once, for by crying out for aid he would anger the bear, who would doubtless try to reach the loft. His only hope was to keep the animal down until his father, or some one else, should come to the cabin to learn the cause of his delay. And even then, — and the boy shuddered to think of it, — whosoever came would be likely to fall a victim to the monster, as no one but himself was aware of its presence. He could not get out of the cabin except by the way he had entered it; and as the bear made that an impossibility, there was no way by which he could alarm the settlers. It was a desperate situation; and, following his first impulse, John lifted up his heart to God, and prayed for deliverance from his danger. All the while he kept his eyes on the bear, watching with the most intense anxiety the animal's every movement. Bruin, however, seemed very sure in his own mind that he would make his dinner on the boy, and sat motionless watching him, and uttering low growls of satisfaction.

The ladder, by means of which John had

climbed into the loft, was made of two oak saplings, with rounds of the same kind of wood fastened into auger holes in the saplings. It rested loosely against the loft, and, as he feared the animal might climb up to him by means of it, John resolved to throw it down into the room below. The bear watched him narrowly, as if half suspecting his intention; and, with his heart beating so violently as almost to suffocate him, John moved back cautiously, and, seizing the ladder with both hands, pushed it slowly and noiselessly along the ground below him, until the top barely rested against the loft. One more vigorous push would have sent the ladder clattering to the earthen floor; but with a sharp growl, the bear at this instant sprang at the rounds, and commenced to mount them. John pushed the saplings with all his might; but the weight of the bear was too much for him, and he could not move the ladder an inch. The monster came nearer, nearer, and the next moment he would be in the loft. John could feel his hot breath, as he struggled awkwardly up the ladder, and he almost fainted with terror and despair. The next moment, however, there was a crash, and the saplings, which had never been designed to withstand such a severe test, broke under the bear's enormous weight, and Bruin and the remnants of the ladder fell heavily to the ground below. The animal lay flat on his back for a moment, looking up at the loft with an expression of bewilderment, at which John, in spite of his alarm, burst into a laugh. Then springing to his feet, the bear uttered a growl of rage, and commenced to run around the room, as if seeking some other means of getting at the boy. John had no weapon but his hunting-knife, which, with boyish pride, he always wore; and he took this out now, resolved that if the bear did reach the loft, he would sell his life as dearly as possible. At this moment his feet struck against something hard, and, stooping down, he picked up a stout club he had put there some time before to season. He felt sure he could give Bruin some hard knocks with this, and he clutched it resolutely, and watched his enemy.

The bear had now paused in his walk, and was looking up at the loft with a puzzled expression. Suddenly he walked over to the opposite side of the cabin, and, running swiftly towards the opening, sprang into the air towards the left, and tried to catch the floor with his paws. He was unsuccessful, however, and fell back upon the floor with a growl.

"O, ho, my fine fellow!" said John; "that's your game — is it? I think I can teach you a trick worth two of that."

Grasping his cudgel in both hands, John stood by the opening, waiting the bear's next leap. It came soon, and this time Bruin's head appeared in the opening on a level with the floor of the loft, which he endeavored to clutch with his claws. Had he been left to himself, he would doubtless have succeeded; but at this instant John's cudgel came crashing down on the monster's head, almost stunning him, and sending him down to the ground again. John uttered a shout of exultation, to which the bear responded with a growl of rage, and again the latter sprang at the loft. This time he succeeded in fastening his claws in the floor, and was trying to draw his immense body up after him, when John, dropping his club, and drawing his hunting-knife, drove the weapon with all his force into the animal's paw. The knife was as keen as a razor, and the blow almost cut the paw from the arm, and Bruin fell back to the ground terribly wounded, and with the blood flowing freely from the cut. Instead of disheartening him, however, his wound made him furious, and he sprang again at the loft, and with such force that it seemed he would enter it. Another blow from John's club sent him back to his starting-place, and the boy answered his growls of fury with mocking laughter. Again and again Bruin essayed the jumping process; but each time John struck him over the head with tremendous force, and at length these blows began to tell even upon so thick a skull as that of the bear, who finally lay still and panting on the ground, evidently very much worsted by his antagonist.

John now received an unexpected reënforcement. The cabin door was standing open, and he saw enter through it the dog he had brought from the Potomac. Carlo was a magnificent specimen of the mastiff breed, and had always been a great pet with the whole family, especially with John, who had taken the care of him upon himself. The dog had evidently been attracted by the growls of the bear, and had come to learn for himself the cause of the strange sounds. As he paused in the doorway, the bear sprang to his feet, and for a moment the two animals gazed at each other. Then, with an angry bark, Carlo sprang at the bear, and Bruin made a dash at the dog. The former had calculated his movements well, and, eluding with great dexterity the blow which the latter aimed at him with his paw, and which would, no doubt, have stunned him, he flew upon the bear, and seized him by the throat, fastening his sharp fangs in the flesh, and making the monster roar with pain. The bear now, finding himself at a disadvantage, clasped his antagonist around the body with his huge paws, and hugged him with such force that it seemed he would crush him, and for several minutes it appeared doubtful who would be victorious.

Since the arrival of the dog, John had watched the scene below him with intense interest. He knew that Carlo would make a good fight, and he was anxious to escape from his dangerous situation. When he saw Carlo seize Bruin by the throat, he knew that the latter would have as much as he could do to shake him off, and he prepared to make his escape from the cabin. The next instant, however, he saw the monster clasp the dog in his arms, and heard poor Carlo, who still held the bear by the throat, utter a faint howl of agony. This decided the boy's course. Not even to save his own life would he abandon his pet to the bear. Throwing his club down, and grasping his knife firmly, he sprang down through the opening to the ground below. As he did so, the bear glared at him with his red, fiendish-looking eyes, and strained the dog closer to him, as if to make short work of him. John picked up his club, and, swinging it in the air, brought it down vigorously upon the bear's skull, repeating his blows with such force and celerity that Bruin roared with rage and pain. He relaxed his hold upon the dog, and struck at John furiously with his wounded paw; but the dog held him fast by the throat, and John skilfully avoided the animal's blows. The cabin now resounded with the howls of the bear, and the boy felt sure that this unusual noise must soon bring assistance, and he redoubled his blows, holding his hunting-knife between his teeth all the time, so that it might be ready for use at any moment.

The bear struggled violently to get away from the dog and seize the boy, and suddenly gave the cudgel a wrench with his paw, tore it from John's hand, and hurled it across the cabin. This was done with such force that it threw the boy off his balance, and before he recovered it, the bear seized him with his wounded paw, and hugged him violently. He now had both the boy and the dog in his arms, and he strained them to him with a terrible force. Carlo still kept his teeth fastened in the bear's neck, and John, whose right hand was free, managed to get his knife in his grasp, and with it he struck the monster repeated blows in the face and neck, bringing the blood at every blow. The struggle went on in this way for fully five minutes longer, and each moment seemed to the boy like an age. The yells of the bear resounded through the cabin, and the blood was flowing from him in half a dozen places; but his immense strength began to tell powerfully in his favor. John felt himself growing fainter every moment, and it seemed that his huge antagonist would win the victory, after all. The pressure of the animal's paw around his body almost suffocated him, and gradually his consciousness began to leave him. He heard, or fancied he heard, a quick, sharp report, like the crack of a rifle, and a loud shout, and then all grew dark to him, and he fainted.

When he recovered his consciousness he was lying on the grass in front of the cabin, with his head resting in his father's lap. Captain Oxenford was chafing his hands, and trying to restore him, while several of the neighbors were looking on anxiously. Dan Whittaker, with his rifle in one hand and a pail of water in the other, was eagerly watching him, and when he saw John open his eyes, he gave a loud shout, and danced about for joy. John was stiff and sore from his encounter with his shaggy foe, and was also very much bruised by the bear's embrace. Fortunately none of his bones were broken, however. The neighbors carried him into the fort, and laid him on his own bed; and it was several days before he was able to be up and at work again. After they carried him into the fort, Dan told him the result of the fight. The loud roars of the monster had alarmed the settlers, and as Dan happened to be the nearest to the cabin, he was the first to ascertain the cause of the noises. Upon seeing his friend in such a desperate situation, he hurried to the fort, and took down John's rifle. Without waiting to answer Mrs. Oxenford's questions as to the cause of his excitement, he rushed back to the cabin, which he reached about the time John fainted. It was but the work of a moment to place the muzzle of his rifle right against the animal's eye, and send a bullet through his brain. The bear fell back dead, and released his hold upon his victims. Just then Captain Oxenford and the rest arrived, and commenced their efforts to restore the brave boy to consciousness.

The bear was an immense animal, and was a rich prize. He had evidently come into the settlement to satisfy his hunger, — a very common circumstance in those days, — and both John and his dog were very fortunate in escaping with their lives. John's story of his encounter with Bruin was told modestly, but it won him praise from all in the settlement; and one of the old hunters told him warmly that he had "the true grit in him," and would do honor to his name yet. Big Dan Whittaker was loud in his praise, and was never tired of questioning his friend about his exploit. He made light of his own share in the affair; but John never forgot that it was Dan's presence of mind that released him so soon from his dangerous position.

As the two boys had killed the bear, it was divided between their families; but these distributed the meat through the whole settlement. The skin was kept as a trophy; and Mrs. Oxenford made each of the boys a cap out of it. They were very proud of these caps, as they had good reason to be, and wore them until they literally fell to pieces.

CHAPTER VI.

AN ADVENTURE WITH THE INDIANS.

THE spring and summer passed away, and the fall, which is nowhere so lovely as in the Ohio Valley, came in its turn. The settlers had heard rumors of hostilities with the Indians, but as yet they had seen none. Whether the savages were in ignorance of the Fish Creek settlement, or whether they had determined to spare it, no one could say; but the perfect immunity from danger which they had enjoyed inclined the settlers to be a little sceptical on the subject of the rumors which reached them. Their doubts were removed, however, about the fifth of September, by a message from Colonel Shepherd, at Fort Fincastle, to Captain Oxenford. The note from the former officer informed the latter that Lord Dunmore was marching towards the Ohio, with an army, to crush the power of the savages, and that orders had been received to put all the frontier posts in a state of defence. The colonel urged the captain to lose no time in getting his neighbors into the fort. A number of Indians had crossed the Ohio in the neighborhood of Grove Creek, and it was well to be prepared for the worst. The settlers lower down the Ohio had already experienced much trouble at the hands of the savages, and it was impossible to tell when or where the next blow would fall. The colonel said that the governor of the colony, Lord Dunmore, would soon be on the frontier with a strong force, as he was already assembling his army on the eastern slope of the Alleghenies, but that until he did arrive the people must take their defence into their own hands.

Colonel Shepherd's letter caused very great anxiety in the settlement, and the statement which he made was confirmed by the report of one of the hunters, who announced that he had on that day seen several Indians in the vicinity of the mouth of Fish Creek. It was decided that the various families comprising the little community should at once move into the cabins assigned to them in the fort, and that the grain and other crops, as soon as harvested, should be stored in the unoccupied cabins, so that they might not be exposed to loss. These things were soon done; the settlers moved into the fort, bringing with them all their household goods and movable property; the animals were quartered in the stables provided for them on the south side of the fort; and in a short time everything was in "apple-pie order." There was an abundance of food in the storehouse, but as each family had its own supplies, there was no necessity for touching the general stock at present.

Captain Oxenford was very strict in enforcing the discipline which he established over the fort. The settlers were required to go to their work beyond the walls armed, and were instructed to return to the fort upon the slightest alarm. The gate was to be kept closed at all times, and was to be placed in charge of a sentinel both night and day. During the day every one, except the younger children, was to pass in and out at will, but at night no one was to leave the fort without permission from the captain. Every person was charged to observe the utmost vigilance and prudence. The hunters were to act as scouts; and, for this purpose, they alone had leave to go and come at will at all hours.

By the time the harvest came, everything in and about the fort was fully arranged, and it presented a very thriving and busy appearance with its ten families. The harvest was gathered in as usual, and the crops belonging to those who lived on the south side of the creek were stored in the fort also. This being done, the settlers began to lay in their usual supply of game.

Thus the early autumn wore away, and still no signs of the Indians were seen about the settlement. The cattle had, up to this time, been turned out to graze occasionally, and thus far no harm had befallen them.

Towards the last of October, news came that Lord Dunmore, who had really *done more* to bring on the war, which is still called by his name in the west, than any other living being, had made peace with the savages; but it was a peace that few had any faith in. The people at Fish Creek determined that they would remain in the fort during the winter, which was now close at hand, and return to their old dwellings in the spring.

The cows were driven up regularly every afternoon about four o'clock, and this duty was generally performed by the older boys. On the day that the news of the peace came, it was John Oxenford's turn to bring in the cattle. This was never a very onerous task, as they were generally but a short distance from the fort. As he started off, John looked for Dan Whittaker to accompany him, but Dan was busy, and could not leave his work.

"Let me go with you, brother," said little Thomas Oxenford. "I can drive the cows as well as Dan Whittaker."

"Come along, then," said John. "You'll soon have to bear your share of this work, and you may as well begin now."

They passed out of the fort, and took their way to the woods. About half a mile from the settlement, and over the hill which lay back of it, was a large meadow, which was the favorite grazing-ground of the cattle, and to that place the boys bent their steps. The season was that delightful Indian summer time, when the Ohio Valley puts on its richest lines of beauty, and when the fascination of its scenery is greater than at any other period of the year. The lads, young as they were, were keenly alive to the beauty of the scene, and they moved along leisurely, gazing upon it in silence. They passed over the brow of the hill and down the northern slope, and reached the edge of the meadow. Just then Thomas burst into a shout of delight.

"Look, John," he cried, pointing to a large tree, but a few feet from them — "look at the chestnuts! Let us stop and gather some."

John felt that it would be wrong to stop for the nuts, as he had been ordered to bring in the cows at once, but the temptation presented by the tree, which was fairly loaded with the delightful fruit, was too great for him; so you see, my dear reader, pioneer boys were quite as apt to neglect business for pleasure as those of the present day. John looked up at the sun, which was still high in the heavens, and, after a moment's hesitation, said,—

"Come, Tom, we must be quick about it, for we haven't got long to be here. You know we must have the cows at the fort by sunset."

"O, it will not take us long to get a few nuts," said Tom. "We can fill our caps, and take them along with us."

The boys then started for the tree. They found a plenty of sticks on the ground, and with these they brought down a large quantity of the nuts, which were perfectly ripe, and as sweet as they could desire. But, instead of filling their caps, and proceeding in their search after the cows, they sat down on a log, and commenced to eat the nuts. They were so much interested in this performance that they were unconscious that the afternoon was passing away rapidly. At last Tom sprang up, and exclaimed, quickly, —

"We'll catch it now, John. Yonder come father and one of the neighbors; and if father finds us here, instead of looking after the cows, he'll make us smoke for it."

John looked in the direction to which his brother pointed, and saw two men approaching them. The new-comers were dressed like the settlers at the fort, and one of them carried a bridle in his hand. The boys commenced looking about very busily, and called the cows with all their might, hoping in this way to disarm their father of his suspicions. In a few minutes the strangers were near enough for them to ascertain their true character, and the boys, to their astonishment and alarm, found that they were in the presence of two large Indians. They were terribly frightened, and started to run away.

"Stop, stop!" cried one of the savages, sharply. "White boy run, Injun shoot. Injun kill."

"Stop, Tom," said John; "they will certainly shoot us if we try to run away. We must go back, and see what they want with us."

The boys then faced about, and walked back hand in hand to where the Indians were standing with their guns levelled at them. As they came up, one of the men seized John by the shoulder, and brandished his tomahawk furiously over his head; but the boy looked him in the face without flinching, and the savage lowered his arm with a grunt of satisfaction.

"Ugh!" he exclaimed, in his broken English, "white boy no 'fraid. Be big chief some day."

"Why should I be afraid of you?" asked John, calmly. "I have never harmed you."

"Injun hate white man," said the warrior, sharply. "Injun no hurt boy. Take him home; make him big chief."

The Indian then told the boys that he and his companion were looking for horses, and that they must go with them. They would not hurt them as long as they submitted to their fate, but if they offered the least resistance, or attempted to escape, they would kill and scalp them. The savages then started off, and, taking a circuitous route over the Fish Creek hills, continued their search after horses.

Thomas was very much frightened by his capture, and kept silence; but John, whose fertile brain had already marked out his line of conduct for him, became quite talkative.

"I'm glad you've taken us," he said to the Indian who could speak English, as they walked along. "I don't want to live in a fort. I want to be a warrior like you, and take lots of scalps."

"Ugh!" grunted the savage, pleased by the compliment, and unsuspicious of the boy's motive.

"Yes," said John, "I'm tired of living in

the fort. My father makes me work hard, and beats me. He never lets me play like other boys, but makes me work like a dog. I want to go with you, and be a great hunter, and a warrior, and live in the woods, and kill deer, and wild turkeys, and buffaloes."

Thomas had listened to his brother in the most profound astonishment. He knew John was not speaking the truth, but he failed to comprehend his motive for the deception; so, when the Indian was telling his companion what John had said, the little fellow whispered to his brother, reproachfully, —

"O, John! you don't mean that — do you?"

"Of course I don't," whispered John, in reply. "You must let me do all the talking, Tom, and mustn't contradict me. I've got a plan on foot, and I want to carry it out."

The Indian now turned to John, and told him he was very glad to hear him talk so, and that he and his companion would carry him and his brother to their people, and make Indians out of them, and that by the time they were grown up they would have no white blood in them. During the afternoon he became very intimate with the lad, and gave him his tomahawk to carry. Thomas, however, said nothing, but kept close to his brother's side all the way.

About sunset the Indians halted at a spring in a hollow, about three miles from the fort. They built a fire, and cooked their supper, which they shared with the boys. John made himself very useful in building the fire, and getting water for his captors, and received many grunts of satisfaction and approval from them. One of them asked him if he knew where they could find any horses; but as he thought it best to tell them the truth this time, he answered that he did not think they would be successful in their search, that the settlers kept their horses up all the time, and never allowed them to run out, for fear the Indians might get them.

After the night had fairly set in, the savages covered up the fire, and tied the boys' hands.

They then made them lie down together, and placed a leather strap or thong over them, and stretched themselves out upon the ends of the strap — one on each side of the boys. They lay awake for a long time, laughing and talking. John, who was a lively fellow, amused his captors with a number of funny stories, which made them laugh heartily. These stories he told to the Indian who could speak English, and that one, in his turn, related them to his companion in their own tongue.

Poor little Thomas, utterly unable to understand his brother's motives for the part he was playing, listened to him in silent indignation. He was once or twice on the point of openly reproaching him for turning against his friends; but, as John had told him to remain quiet, he concluded that it was best for him to do so. Still, he could not understand why John should be so well pleased at their capture, or why he should want to be an Indian; and the more he thought of it, the harder he found the attempt to understand his brother's conduct. John soon increased his perplexity; for when the Indian, who had been the spokesman, was engaged in telling his companion a story John had just told him, the boy whispered softly to his little brother, —

"I say, Tom, don't you go to sleep to-night. Stay awake if you ever wish to see home again; and, above all things, hold your tongue."

John Oxenford was merely carrying out a plan which he had conceived immediately after his capture. He had heard from the hunters at the fort many a story of border warfare, and as soon as he was made a prisoner he resolved to escape. This was his reason for telling his brother to say nothing, and let him do all the talking; and he had spent all the afternoon in trying to make friends of the savages, and lull their suspicions to rest. He knew his brother would not understand his motives for acting as he did, but he could not tell him without revealing everything to the Indian who could speak English, and in this way ruining their chance for escape. After the savages tied him and made him lie down for the night, his courage almost failed him. The Indians, as I have said, had placed their leather strap over the boys, and were lying upon the ends of it themselves, so that any attempt on the part of the prisoners to get up on their feet would move the strap and wake their captors. The situation seemed hopeless enough, but John determined to wait patiently and see if something more favorable did not happen; and, as he always did in times of danger and trouble, he prayed for "deliverance from on high." After the Indians ceased talking, he lay silently thinking over the plan he had resolved upon. He believed that the Indians had no fear of his trying to leave them, as they had faith in the story he had told them; but how he should get out of their power he could not tell. Something must be done that night. He knew the spot where they were resting, and could eastly find his way back to the fort; but the next day the

Indians would strike across the country towards their own settlements, and even should they succeed in escaping during the journey, there was a strong probability of their being retaken and killed, or of losing their way and dying of starvation, or of wandering into an Indian camp. The necessity, therefore, for doing something that night, was imperative.

The boy's mind was busy with these thoughts, but he knew that it was useless to make even the slightest attempt as long as the Indians were awake. The suspense in which he was placed, was painful, and, in spite of the chilliness of the night, the thick sweat stood heavy on his forehead. At last the heavy breathing of the savages convinced him that they were asleep; but as he could not move without awaking them, his situation was not bettered by their unconsciousness.

The night was very chilly, and in about an hour after the savages fell asleep, one of them, becoming cold, lifted John in his arms, and rolled him on the outside, settled himself in the boy's place, and was soon breathing heavily again. This was just what the lad wanted, but what he had not dared to hope for. The Indian had put him where he could move without disturbing the others, and had not only removed the strap from him, but had rolled off from it himself. Profiting by this, the boy slowly and cautiously rolled away from his companions, and commenced trying to undo the thongs with which his hands were tied. Fortunately for him, the Indians had not fastened him very securely. He worked slowly and softly — so slowly indeed, that it seemed he would never free himself. Every motion seemed to his excited imagination more violent than was prudent, and he was tormented with the fear that the Indians would suddenly awake, and discover his attempt to escape. In such a case he felt sure they would kill him. The time wore away very slowly, but at length he succeeded in removing his fetters, and, rising gently to his feet, he looked around to assure himself that all was well.

The huge forms of the Indians were stretched out at full length, and their heavy, regular breathing convinced him that they were still sound asleep. Another glance showed him the great round blue eyes of his little brother Thomas, watching his movements with the most intense eagerness. He placed his finger warningly upon his lips to caution the little fellow not to move or make any sound that might disturb the savages, and then, stepping cautiously to his brother's side, he raised the strap softly, and signed to the boy to get up on his feet. The astonished Thomas obeyed him, and John led him noiselessly a few feet away from the sleepers, and commenced to untie his hands. How their hearts throbbed as they stood there in the dark woods, with danger and death so near them! The very sighing of the night wind, the rustling of the leaves, and the murmuring of the waters of the little stream by which they had encamped, made them start and tremble with fear. The slightest sound might arouse their captors, and then, poor boys, home and a mother's face would never gladden their eyes again.

At last Tom's hands were freed, and the little fellow, intent only upon getting off safe, whispered to his brother,—

"Come now, brother John, let us run home as fast as we can."

John knew this would never do. Tom would be sure to arouse the savages in attempting to run away, and, as the little fellow had already turned to put his proposal into execution, he seized him firmly by the shoulder, and whispered to him,—

"Don't run away yet, Tom. If you do, you'll wake the Indians, and they'll be sure to kill us. You mustn't stir yet, for we must kill these Indians before we go."

"We are not big enough to kill them," said Tom, trembling at the thought.

"We've got it to do, or be killed ourselves," whispered John. "You must do your share."

Tom looked at the great, stalwart warriors

that lay sleeping at his feet, and for the life of him he could not see how two such boys as they were could hope to prevail against them. His brother whispered to him that they had no time to lose, and, yielding to him, Tom expressed his readiness to do what he could.

The plan upon which John determined would have done credit to an old Indian hunter. It exhibited an unusual degree of fertility of resource, as well as the most determined courage. Stealing noiselessly up to the Indians, he took one of their rifles, which was loaded and primed, and, cocking it, placed it on a log, with the muzzle only an inch or two from the head of one of the sleepers. He then stationed Tom at the breech of the weapon, and made him put his finger on the trigger, and told him to pull the trigger and shoot the savage, as soon as he should strike the other. Then, stepping back, he possessed himself of the Indian's tomahawk, having found that it would be impossible to remove the rifle without disturbing its owner. He grasped the tomahawk firmly, and then, assuring himself by a glance that his youngest brother was ready, he stepped softly to the sleepers, and placed himself astride of one of them. They were still unconscious, the fatigue of their long journey during the previous day having thrown them into a profound slumber. The boy raised the tomahawk with both hands, and, concentrating all his energies in the blow, struck the savage with it. The blow fell upon the back of the Indian's neck, and a little to the side, so as not to be fatal. Half stunned, the savage attempted to spring up and defend himself, but John struck him on the head. Even this blow, though it cut through the skull with a horrible crash, did not kill the man; but the boy, rendered desperate by the gravity of his situation, struck him so fast, so often, and with such fatal effect, that, as the lad afterwards expressed it himself, the Indian "lay still, and began to quiver." In another moment the huge savage lay motionless at his feet, and, having satisfied himself that there was nothing more to apprehend from this one, John turned to see what disposition his brother had made of the other.

Tom had also done his part well. As soon as he saw his elder brother strike the Indian, he pulled the trigger and discharged the rifle. The ball struck the sleeping savage in the face, and tore away a considerable part of his lower jaw, and the Indian, a few moments after receiving the shot, began to flounce about and yell in the most terrible manner. He was so completely startled by the suddenness of the attack, that he did not for a moment attribute it to his captives, and his wound was so terrible as to utterly deprive him, for a time, of the power of resistance. As soon as he had fired, Tom dropped the rifle, and hurried over to where his brother was standing.

All this had taken scarcely as much time as I have consumed in telling it, and the boys at once set off for the fort at full speed. In spite of their efforts, however, they travelled slow, for it was very difficult to find their way in the darkness. They feared that they had not killed the other Indian, and that he would pursue them and murder them; and the breaking of every twig under their feet, the rustle of every leaf, made them tremble with alarm.

At last they came in sight of the clearing around the settlement, and John could see by the brightening of the clouds in the east that the day would soon break. They could see the dark outline of the fort, about half a mile beyond them; but everything was as still as death, and with beating hearts they set off at a run. They reached the gate almost out of breath, and knocked loudly upon it. The sentinel on duty was none other than Dan Whittaker, and the boy was about half asleep.

"Who's that out there?" he called, drowsily.

"It's me. Open the gate," cried John, breathlessly.

"And who's me?" asked Dan, growing wider awake.

"John Oxenford," was the reply. "Open

the gate quick, Dan, if it's you. The Indians may be after us at any moment."

Dan gave a great whoop, and the bars which closed the entrance came clattering to the ground, and the heavy gate swung open. Dan caught his friend in his arms, and gave him a great hug. He could not leave his post, but told the boys they would find their parents in the block-house, to which they at once proceeded.

They found all the neighbors gathered in their father's cabin, endeavoring to console and cheer their parents. Their absence had occasioned the greatest alarm and anxiety in the fort, as none of the parties that had gone out to look for them had been able to learn anything of them. They found their mother with her head lying in her husband's lap, sobbing bitterly, while Captain Oxenford bent over her, utterly incapable of offering her any consolation, so greatly was he in need of it himself.

"Poor boys, poor boys!" sobbed the mother. "They are killed or taken prisoners by the Indians, and I shall never see them again."

John's heart was in his throat as he heard his mother's grief; but he burst into the room, half laughing, half crying, followed by Tom, who was blubbering outright.

"No, mother," cried the boys; "we are not dead, and here we are."

You may be sure, dear reader, the lads had a warm welcome from all present, and their parents' grief was changed into the deepest joy. After the excitement produced by their arrival had subsided, John told the story of their capture and escape, not even concealing their misconduct in stopping to gather the chestnuts. When he described the manner in which they had killed and wounded the Indians, one of the old hunters, who was present, gave a long whistle.

"Whew, lad!" he exclaimed, incredulously; "that's a very fine tale you've told, but it's a pretty hard one. You and your dog thar may be pretty good at a bar fight; but I don't know any Injuns you could have licked as easy as that."

"I've told the truth," said John, flushing. "Whether you believe it or not, everything happened as I have said."

"Don't git riled, my boy," said the hunter, kindly. "You hain't got a better friend in the fort than me, and I'd be powerful glad if I could believe your yarn; but I'm too old an Injun-fighter for that."

"Well, then, Bill Davis," said John, sharply, "I'll prove that I speak the truth. It will be broad day in a few minutes, and as soon as the sun rises I'll go with you, and show you the place."

"Done," said the hunter; "and if I'm wrong, my boy, I'll ax your pardon with all my heart."

Breakfast was made ready early, and as soon as it was despatched, a party of six or seven, consisting of Captain Oxenford, Bill Davis, Dan Whittaker, and several others, left the fort, under John's guidance, to ascertain the truth of the boy's story. Captain Oxenford had never known his son to tell a lie, and he was very anxious that John's veracity should be sustained by the result of the investigation. He cared very little for the credit which would be gained by his boys for their exploit. He was chiefly anxious to show the settlers that they had not lied. John guided the party by the shortest route, and they soon stood upon the spot which had been the scene of the last night's tragedy.

The Indian he had tomahawked lay on the ground, stiff and cold in death, but the other one, who had been wounded by the discharge of the rifle, had crawled away from the camp, and had taken his gun and shot-pouch with him. The evidence afforded by the dead Indian was indisputable, and the boy pointed to him with an air of triumph, and, turning to the hunter, exclaimed, proudly, —

"Well, Bill Davis, what do you say now?"

"I say," said the hunter, warmly, seizing John's hand, and wringing it in his vice-like grasp, "I say that, boy as you are, you are the best man in the fort, and I ax your pardon, lad, for doubting your story just now; but you see it was hard for an old hunter, like me, to believe that two shavers, like you and Tom, could lick two of the best warriors in the whole Shawnee tribe."

"Then you know this Indian, Davis?" said Captain Oxenford.

"Know him, cap'n?" replied the hunter. "You jist bet I do. He's shot at me often, and we hunted each other for a whole year once, but somehow both of us came out safe, and we gave up the chase. He was a 'big Injun,' as the red-skins call their braves, and I reckon his pardner was one of the same stripe."

As he spoke, the old man drew his hunting-knife from its sheath, and tried its edge on his finger; then, before his companions really knew what he was about, he bent over the dead savage, and cut his scalp off. Raising the gory trophy, he handed it to John.

"Here's your prize, lad," he said, holding out the scalp. "What! don't want it?" he added, laughing, as he saw the boy shrink back in horror. "You've earned it fairly. Well, it does you credit, anyhow, and I'll keep it and dry it for you. If these troubles last as long as I think they will, you'll be proud of this here har yet."

And, so saying, the hunter commenced to prepare the scalp for carrying, by taking it to the brook, and washing the blood from it.

"Now," said Captain Oxenford, "let us see what has become of the other Indian."

They followed the trail made by the wounded savage, and found him lodged in the branches of a large tree, which had fallen to the ground, about a quarter of a mile from the camp. Notwithstanding the severity of his wound, which was gradually producing lockjaw, the Indian was resolved to sell his life as dearly as possible. Bracing himself in the tree, with the strength of despair, the savage rested his gun on one of the limbs, and taking aim at the foremost man of the party, pulled the trigger; but, fortunately, his gun missed fire. The white men heard the snap of the lock, and made a simultaneous movement backward.

"Hang me," muttered the old hunter, "if I want to be shot by a dead Injun. I'll fix his flint for him."

Raising his rifle, the old man aimed it deliberately at the savage, and fired, and the next moment the fellow fell to the ground a corpse.

"Thar," said Davis, bending over him, and scalping him, "I thought I knowed him. The Shawnees will miss you, my fine fellows, and, if I ain't much mistaken, they'll do thar best to get some of our har to pay for yours."

The rifles and ammunition of the Indians were secured, and the party went back to the fort. John's story was now fully sustained, and old Bill Davis, who had been the first to doubt the boys, was now loudest in their praise, in which the whole community joined right heartily. Tom came in for his share too, and it was decided by the men that the two rifles, which had been taken from the Indians, should

8

be given to the boys. John was old enough to use his, and Tom's was put away until he should be large enough to handle it. The weapons were of the best quality, and were very valuable, and in the long war which followed these occurrences, they did good service.

CHAPTER VII.

THE "TOMAHAWK RIGHT."

"JOHN," said Captain Oxenford, one morning, "do you think you can make a sweep for the hominy block?"

"I can try it, sir," was the reply. "But where shall I put it?"

"It is for the benefit of the whole settlement," said the captain, "and you'll have to put it where all can get at it easily. I reckon you'd better put it at the south end of the storehouse."

John set to work at once. He cut down a small sugar tree, and trimmed off a pole from it about thirty feet long. This he dragged into the fort with the aid of one of the horses, and fastened the but-end under the lower layer of logs in the storehouse. Two forks were then driven into the ground at about one third the length of the pole, in order to support it firmly, and elevate the small end about fifteen feet from the ground. To the small end of this pole was attached, by a large mortise, a piece of sapling about five or six inches in diameter, and eight or ten feet long, the lower end of which was shaped to answer for a pestle. A pin of wood was then put through the pestle at the proper height, so that two persons could work the sweep at once. Under the pestle the hominy block was placed, and this consisted of a large block of wood about three feet long, with an excavation burned at one end, wide at the top, and narrow at the bottom, so that the action of the pestle on the bottom threw the corn up to the sides towards the top of it, from whence it continually fell down into the centre. The sapling being very elastic, the work of pounding the corn into hominy or meal was very much lightened by means of this sweep.

John did his work well, and in the course of a few hours the sweep was in operation. It was kept going almost constantly, for it was the sole dependence of ten families. The corn was beaten as fine as a succession of heavy blows could break it, and the mass was then bolted through a sifter made of a piece of fine deer-skin stretched over a hoop, the holes being perforated with a small hot wire. That which passed through the holes was meal, and was used for making bread, while the coarser pieces were boiled as hominy.

The winter wore away monotonously, for there was nothing to afford amusement to the dwellers in the fort at such a time; but towards the close of it, an incident occurred which gave a little variety to the humdrum character of the life they led.

It was late in January, 1775, and towards the close of a remarkably cold day, that a stranger, mounted on a very rough-looking horse, reached the fort from the direction of Wheeling. He rode up to the enclosure, and asked permission to spend the night there, which was cordially given by Captain Oxenford, and the man was admitted within the walls, and his horse put away in the stable. He made himself very agreeable during the evening, and gave the latest news from the colonies east of the mountains, which information the settlers considered ample remuneration for all the extra trouble his visit caused them. The next morning, however, the stranger was not quite so agreeable. He informed Captain Oxenford that he was the owner of the land on which the little settlement was located, and that he had come out for the purpose of arranging his claims with the settlers. He said he was disposed to sell the land at a very low figure, and that, as the settlers had been to considerable trouble to improve the land, he supposed they would rather pay for it than move away.

Captain Oxenford listened to him in silence, his indignation and surprise at the fellow's impudence rendering him speechless.

"What do you mean by claiming to be the owner of this land?" he asked, at length. "We found it unoccupied, and we claim it by right of having settled it."

"That's very true, cap'," said the man; "but you see I spotted this here tract before you did."

"Then you should have settled on it," said the captain, indignantly. "As you failed to do so, you have no claim upon it."

"Wait a bit and I'll show you," said the man, insolently. "Three years ago I came here, and saw this valley. I made up my mind that I had better lay claim to it, as some one would be likely to settle here. I took my tomahawk and deadened a few trees about the spring out yonder. Then I cut my initials, 'P. P.,' which stand for Paul Payson; that's my name, cap'; and, according to the rules here on the border, that gives me a 'tomahawk right' to this land." *

* Doddridge says, in his "Notes on Western Virginia,"—

"I remember having seen a number of those 'tomahawk rights' when a boy. For a long time many of them bore the names of those who made them. I have no knowledge of the efficacy of the tomahawk improvement, or whether it conferred any right whatever, unless followed by an actual settlement. These rights, however, were often bought and sold. Those who wished to make settlements . . . often

"Suppose we refuse to recognize your right — what then?" asked the captain, controlling his anger.

"Well, then," said the man, impudently, "I'll go up to Wheeling, and get a posse of men, and put you off."

"You'll find no one there base enough to aid you," said the captain; "and besides, you have no law to justify you."

"There's no law on the subject, I know," said the man; "but it's a custom here on the border, and I mean to carry it out. I've come here to settle the thing peaceably; but if you mean to show fight, why, I can show it, too."

"Mr. Payson," said Captain Oxenford, sternly, "your claim is infamous. By your own

bought up the tomahawk improvements, rather than enter into quarrels with those who had made them. Other improvers of the land, . . . who happened to be stout, veteran fellows, took a very different course from that of purchasing the 'tomahawk rights.' When annoyed by the claimants under those rights, they deliberately cut a few good hickories, and gave them what was called in those days 'a laced jacket;' that is, a sound whipping."

confession, you had a whole year in which to settle this land before we came. You threw away your opportunity, and we have had the toil and trouble necessary to the redemption of this valley from the wilderness. We refuse to recognize your bogus claim, and base our rights upon our actual settlement. You can bring as many men here as you please; but if they interfere with us, we shall drive them away. We will defend our rights with our lives."

"Then you are a parcel of thieves," began Payson, angrily; but the captain cut him short.

"Look you, my man," said he, his eyes flashing, "you had better hold your tongue. A repetition of your words will bring down upon you the punishment you merit."

By this time nearly all the settlers had collected on the spot where the conversation was being held, which was just outside of the gate of the fort, and they demanded eagerly to know the cause of the quarrel, for such they perceived it to be.

"This man," said Captain Oxenford, "has come here to demand that we shall buy from him the land we have earned by our labor and privations. He says he has a tomahawk right to it, as he saw it three years ago, and cut his initials on the trees around the spring yonder. I have told him that we will not recognize such an infamous claim, and he threatens to bring a posse of men here to expel us."

"Sculp him!" cried old Bill Davis, the hunter, whose ideas of retribution were very much like those of the Indians themselves. "Blarst him, I'd like to have his har; I'd put it alongside o' that Injun's sculp John killed t'other day."

It was evident that the settlers were very much inclined to take the old man's advice. Big Dan Whittaker said nothing, but, giving John Oxenford a wink, which the lad understood, stepped over to a grove of young saplings, and cut a stout switch with his knife. He was back in a minute, and set to work to trim the switch in silence. The owner of the "tomahawk right" began to see that he was in considerable danger; but putting on a bold appearance, he declared his intention to maintain his rights to the last.

"Duck him in the creek," cried several of the men. "He's a blackguard; he's no better than a common thief."

There was a movement towards the man, who turned pale, and looked about for a chance to escape; but Captain Oxenford stopped the excited settlers by stepping before the man.

"Don't touch him, men," he said. "Let us show him fair play."

Dan Whittaker had now finished trimming his switch, and, shutting his knife and putting it away, he walked up to the trembling sharper.

"Let me settle his claim, captain," he said. "We are a good match."

"Well, then, if you will have it so, Dan," said the captain, who saw that this was the only way of saving the man from the wrath of the settlers, and who was really not sorry to see the matter so adjusted, "I have nothing more to say. After all, the fellow deserves some kind of punishment for his insolence."

Stepping aside, he left Dan confronting the man, who was by this time very much frightened.

"You've come here to settle your 'tomahawk right,' I hear," said Dan, mockingly. "Well, old fellow, the way we settle those things is just so."

Seizing the man by the collar, he rained blows fast and heavy on the fellow's back and shoulders. The man struggled hard to get away from him, but Dan held him fast, and flogged him soundly, amid the cheers and yells of the delighted spectators. At last, when fairly out of breath, he released him.

"Now," said Captain Oxenford, to the crest-fallen sharper, "the sooner you get away from here, the better for you."

The man walked silently into the fort, and, taking his horse from the stable, rode out of the enclosure. He paused as he reached the spot where the settlers were still standing, and pointing his finger at Dan Whittaker, he said, or rather lisped, in a tone of the bitterest hatred, —

"You've had your turn to-day, youngster. It'll be my time next, and you mark me if I don't have your life by this time next year."

"You can have a trial at it now, if you'll get down off that horse," said Dan, coolly.

The man tried to speak, but his voice was too unsteady to trust himself; so, darting upon the boy a look of hatred, he put spurs to his horse, and rode off swiftly. Dan burst into a laugh, and turned carelessly away. As he did so, he felt some one touch him on his arm, and, turning, he saw his friend, the old hunter.

"You may laugh, Dan," said the old man, gravely, "but take my word for it, that fellow means what he says. He'll be sure to try to do you some mischief, and I'd be on my guard if I were you."

"I'm not afraid of him," replied Dan. "He's a vile coward, or he never would have let me flog him just now."

"Of course he's a coward," said the hunter, "and that's the reason why I warn you agin him. If he was a brave man, he'd seek no mean advantage over you; but he'll not hesitate to waylay you whenever he can; so take my advice, lad, and be on the watch for him."

The hunter's warning was based upon a keen knowledge of human nature, as seen in that part of the world, and Dan concluded to be influenced by it. His caution, however, was useless, for Payson was never seen or heard of in the neighborhood of Fish Creek again. His "tomahawk right" had been completely settled, and the settlers were troubled with it no more. It was afterwards ascertained that he did not return to Wheeling, as he had threatened. Such a course would have been useless, for the settlers at that post would have laughed at his claim, and he would have stood a good chance of a worse punishment than he met at the hands of Dan Whittaker. As his disappearance left no trace of him behind, the settlers came to believe, with the old hunter, that the Indians had "gobbled him up." It was some time before they ceased to discuss the fellow's visit to them, and to the last their indignation remained as violent as it was on the day of the occurrence.

In the woods just back of the settlement were a number of fine sugar-maple trees. It was the next thing to impossible to obtain sugar on the western side of the mountains, and many months had elapsed since our settlers had seen any. It was proposed by some one to tap the maple trees for sap, and make their own sugar. This would place within their reach an abundant supply of a most delightful quality of sugar. They would be dependent no longer upon the east in this respect, and the plan was so promising that it was decided to try it. The work was to be done in common, and the sugar divided among the families according to their number. Preparations were immediately commenced, and as the winter gave place to the spring, the process of collecting the sap from the trees was begun. Each tree was bored with a medium-sized auger, and into the hole thus made a piece of wood hollowed like a spout was driven. The sap collected in these spouts, and ran slowly into buckets and pails, which were set to catch it. A number of buckets and barrels were made for the occasion, for, among the other accomplishments which their necessities had taught them, some of the settlers had become excellent coopers. As fast as the buckets were filled, they were emptied into the barrels, and in this way a considerable quantity of the sap was collected. In ten days enough had been drawn to enable the settlers to commence boiling the sirup into sugar. Four large fires were kindled in the woods, and over each one was placed a large iron kettle, holding about ten or twelve gallons. The women attended to the boiling, and the men kept the fires supplied with fuel.

This was continued for about a month, at the end of which time it was found that quite a large quantity of sugar and molasses had been made, and it was believed that, with careful economy, the supply could be made to last until the next spring.

My readers must not suppose that the little frontier settlement to which I have devoted these pages was by any means an earthly Paradise. It was like all others of its kind, a collection of plain, rough cabins, inhabited by a rugged, hard-fisted set of people. The privations and hardships endured by the settlers were such as we of to-day can scarcely realize, not the least of which was the severe toil attendant upon clearing up the land and getting in the crops. Almost everything had to be created, and nothing but the direst necessity could have called into such active use the ingenuity that was manifested by nearly every person to supply the deficiencies. Yet, in spite of their hard life, the settlers were contented and happy. They established homes for themselves and their families; they owed no man anything, and they knew that, when they came to die, their children would have an ample inheritance. They felt that the Indians would be steadily driven farther west, and the country more thickly settled, and that their children would reap the reward of their labors, if they did not live to do so themselves.

CHAPTER VIII.

BORDER WAR.

WITH the summer of 1775 came the news of the troubles with England, which were convulsing the whole country. The efforts which the mother country was making to reduce the rebellious colonies to submission were tolerably well understood on the Ohio, in spite of the great difficulties of obtaining authentic information, and the measures of the patriots for resistance found a sympathizer in almost every settler west of the mountains. So rare, indeed, was a Tory found in that region, that the name was scarcely known.

The people of Western Virginia had good cause to be indignant at the conduct of the British authorities, for they had good proof that the mother country was prepared to bring upon them the worst of evils. For some time they had had cause to suspect that the infamous governor of Virginia, Lord Dunmore, had been in negotiation with the Indians for the destruction, by the latter, of the frontier settlements, and in the fall of 1775 they had positive proof of this in the discovery of the plot known as "Connelly's conspiracy;" and the next year, the war having assumed a general character east of the mountains, the struggle began in earnest west of them, between the whites and the savages. Great Britain had taken the latter regularly into her employ, and, to her eternal shame, had offered a reward for every scalp which the savages brought to her military posts along the great lakes. Detroit was her principal stronghold in this region, and that city was the great market for the scalps of the patriots. The war was bitter and merciless.

As soon as the war began, the settlers on Fish Creek, who had left the fort in the spring, after the close of "Dunmore's war," and moved back to their cabins, returned to their quarters in the fort. They hoped the struggle would soon pass by, for they had no conception of its magnitude; but as the time wore on, the savages became more troublesome, and they began to see that they would be compelled to remain in the fort, at least until peace was proclaimed, and when that would be, no one could tell. They heard, towards the close of the summer of 1776, that the colonies had declared themselves absolved from their allegiance to Great Britain; but, as they had never troubled themselves much about that country, they were somewhat at a loss to understand how this separation benefited them. Still, as they regarded England as the author of their troubles with the Indians, they were, on the whole, rather glad that the country was to have no further connection with her.

As late as the fall of 1776 the settlement was exempt from the depredations of the savages, but with the latter part of the harvest it began to take its share in the struggle through which the whole country was passing.

The harvest was almost over. The corn had been gathered in, and was safely stowed away in the fort, and a large part of the fodder had been secured in the same manner. Two days more, and everything would be safe under shelter. It was near sunset, and the settlers, with the exception of two men who had been left to mind the gate, were busy at work in the cornfield. In accordance with the orders of Captain Oxenford, each man had his rifle with him, and, as the hunters had reported signs of Indians in the vicinity of the river on the previous day, each man had his weapon slung across his back by means of a cord of deer-skin, so that it could be ready for use at any moment. The field on the south shore of the creek had been harvested, and all the men were collected in the bottom, which lay within a few hundred yards of the fort. The upper end of this field was bounded by a strip of woods, and it was near this thicket that the men were working when the incident which follows occurred.

John Oxenford — who was now over seventeen years old — and Dan Whittaker were nearest the belt of wood, and were busily engaged in carrying the bundles of fodder to the large stack from which it was to be carried to the fort the next day. Suddenly Dan's quick ear caught the sound of something moving among the trees.

"I say, John," he said, in a low tone, "there's something moving in the woods. I shouldn't be surprised if it is an Indian, or a dozen of them, maybe."

"Let's give the alarm, then," said John, quickly.

"But we don't know that the noise is caused by the approach of the red-skins," said Dan. "It may be a fox, or a bear, or even a squirrel; and if we give the alarm, we shall be laughed at for being frightened."

"I'll take the risk, anyhow," said John. "Father," he cried, running to the captain, who was but a short distance from them, "there are Indians in the woods."

He had scarcely spoken when the reports of ten or twelve rifles rang out from the trees. Fortunately, no one was killed. One of the settlers received a slight wound in the arm, but no damage of a serious nature was done by the volley.

"Run for the fort, men! Run for the fort!" shouted Captain Oxenford. "It is our only hope of safety."

The next moment the whites had unslung their guns from their shoulders, and started for the fort. Orders had been given that day to allow none of the women and children to pass beyond the walls, and the men who had been working in the field were the only persons exposed to the danger. The savages, some eight or ten in number, had counted on surprising the whites; and, as soon as they fired, they sprang from the woods with a loud yell, and dashed towards them. The fugitives were about fifty yards in advance, but the race was a close one, for the red-skins were better runners than their adversaries. Seeing that the Indians were gaining upon them, Captain Oxenford called to his men to halt, discharge their rifles at the enemy, and then resume their efforts to reach the fort; and, suiting the action to the word, he paused, raised his rifle, fired, and ran towards the gate. A yell of pain from the Indians told him that he had struck one of the dusky warriors. Several other shots were fired, one of which wounded another Indian; but the majority of the settlers made no effort to execute the captain's orders, being anxious only to get into the fort alive. The firing had the effect of bringing the Indians to a halt; and taking advantage of this, the settlers got into the enclosure safely. The sentinels at the gate had been startled by the reports of the Indians' rifles, and had at once prepared to admit their friends. The whites once inside the walls, the gates were closed and securely barred. The wounded man had not been very much injured, and he was turned over to the care of the women, while the others proceeded to man the side of the fort nearest the savages.

John Oxenford and Dan Whittaker were eager for a shot at the enemy, and as soon as they got into the fort, they hastened to the block-house overlooking the ground occupied by the savages. The Indians were still standing in the field, huddled around the two who had been wounded. As the boys reached the block-house, they saw them lift the form of one of the wounded men from the ground, preparatory to carrying him off. As they did so, they shook their clinched hands at the fort, and uttered a series of deafening yells.

"They are going off, Dan," said John, as he watched them through a loop-hole. "If we want to get a crack at them, we must be quick about it."

"It's a long distance, John," said Dan, "and I hardly think we can reach them."

"We can try it," said John. "So here goes."

The boys raised their guns, and, passing them through the loop-holes, aimed carefully at the dusky group. The Indians were some distance off, and it was a very doubtful venture the lads were attempting. They aimed slowly and carefully, and fired simultaneously. One of the Indians sprang into the air, and fell to the ground a corpse; but, as the boys had fired together, it was impossible to tell which had killed him. The boys gave a cheer as they saw him fall, and the savages, with a yell, dropped their wounded comrade, and scampered off to the woods, from which they fired several shots at the fort, all of which fell short, however. Several of the settlers, among whom was Captain Oxenford, now came into the block-house.

"Who fired those shots?" asked the captain.

"We did, sir," replied both the boys.

"Didn't you remember my orders about wasting your ammunition?" asked the captain, sternly.

"We didn't waste it, sir," said Dan, eagerly. "We killed an Indian. See," he added, pointing through the loop-hole, "you can see him lying yonder by that big stump. That other fellow is only wounded."

"Don't throw away a shot, boys," said the captain, patting Dan approvingly on the back. "We had better not fire on them again until they make another attack. Do you think they will attempt an attack on the fort to-night?" he asked, turning to Bill Davis, the old hunter, who was their great authority upon Indian matters.

"No, cap'," was the reply; "the varmints ain't strong enough for that. They hoped to surprise us; but as they haven't done so, they'll never risk buttin' thar heads agin these log walls. They've got too much sense for that. They'll stay about here till after dark, so they can carry off them men lyin' yonder; and maybe they'll try to set the fort on fire during the night. We'll have to keep a sharp lookout; but I don't think we need fear anything from them."

"Do you think they will retreat by morning?" asked John.

"P'r'aps so," replied the hunter; "but thar's no tellin'. They may hang around here two or three days, hoping to cut off some straggler from the fort; so you'll have to keep your people up pretty close for a while, cap'; but I can't say what they intend doin'. They're queer critters, them Injuns."

Acting upon the advice of the old hunter, Captain Oxenford gave orders that a strict watch should be kept over all parts of the fort during the night; and for this purpose one man was stationed in each block-house, and one at the gate, while the rest of those who were able to handle a weapon were held in readiness for any emergency in one of the cabins on the side nearest the enemy. The savages remained quiet, however, and in a short time the darkness came on.

It was a very cool night, and the men were given permission to build a fire in the cabin where they were assembled. Their suppers were brought to them by their wives and children, and when this meal was over, they remained in the cabin, awaiting the movements of the Indians. Some were gathered around the fire talking, while others were stretched out on the floor, smoking silently their corn-cob pipes. The fire threw a warm, rich glow over the rugged scene, bringing out every detail in the most picturesque style. Bill Davis was in his element. Seated in one corner of the huge fireplace, he was telling his hearers tales of his experience as an Indian-fighter. John Oxenford, who had become a sort of pet with him since the affair with the Indians, two years before, was lying on the floor, with his head resting against the old man's knee, and Dan Whittaker was standing in the shade of the fireplace, leaning against the wall, and resting both hands on his rifle. Both boys were listening eagerly to the hunter's story; for Achilles himself was never greater in the estimation of those "who warred against Troy," than was Bill Davis in the eyes of these pioneer boys.

"Yes," said the old man, knocking the ashes

from his pipe, preparatory to filling it again, "I led a wild, venturesome life before I came to this here settlement, and I don't know how soon I may go at it again, for I'm pretty tired of bein' cooped up in a pen; but whatever I do, lad," he added, patting John softly on the head, "I'll make this fort my stopping-place, and I'll be here off and on, for I mean to keep an eye on you as long as I live, for I know you'll make your mark yet."

"Thank you, Bill," said John, touched by the hunter's affection for him. "I should be very sorry to have you leave us, and I don't see why you should, for everybody here likes you, and I should be real lonesome without you, and so would Dan."

"I know, lad," said the hunter, softly; "I know. I'll stay as long as I can; but I'm afeard I shan't be able to hold out, for I feel a kind of longin' to be out in the woods agin. But," he added, quickly, "that ain't tellin' you about that fight I had with the Injuns four years ago."

"Let us have it," cried several voices. "We won't interrupt you this time, Bill."

"Very good," said the hunter. "You can question me when I git through, if you want to; but you must let me tell the story without botherin' me, or I can't tell it at all. You see," he began, lighting his pipe, "four years ago there warn't no settlements along the Ohio, except at Wheeling, and on Buffalo and Short Creeks, which lie above Wheeling. The settlements hadn't come down this far, and were scattered along the Monongehela country towards Pennsylvania and Maryland. Very few people had ventured to come over the mountains, and the country west of them was pretty much a wilderness. The Injuns had left it and gone across the Ohio, but they still hunted along it, and this made our people somewhat timid. Well, a party of settlers had located near the head of the North Branch of the Potomac, and had built 'em a block-house, which wasn't a circumstance to this fort, but which did pretty well as a defence agin the

Surprise of Bill Davis. Page 145.

red-skins. I used to hunt in this region, and I made the block-house my headquarters.

"One day, just four years ago this fall, I was riding along a path which led to the settlement, when I came across a vine full of wild grapes. The vine was just loaded down with the fruit, and the grapes looked so luscious that I couldn't make up my mind to pass 'em by; so I rode up under the vine, and in a few minutes I had filled my cap with the grapes. Swingin' my rifle across the pommel of my saddle, I held the cap in my hand, and rode along slowly towards the block-house, eating the grapes as I went along. I hadn't an idea that there was danger about, for I hadn't seen the least sign of an Injun during the whole day; but just as I had got my mouth full of the grapes, and was spitting out the stones and skins, I heard two rifles crack within a dozen yards of me, one on each side of the road. One of the balls cut through my hunting-shirt, and grazed my breast, and the other struck my horse just back of the saddle, and brought him down in his tracks. You may be pretty sure I was astonished, and I come near choking with the grapes I had in my mouth. I fell with my horse; but the next minute I was on my feet, with my rifle in my hand. I might have run away, for I was pretty good at a foot-race; but I couldn't bear to have it said that I ran from only two Injuns. I was bound to bring down one of 'em, at any rate.

"As I jumped on my feet, after the fall of my horse, I heard a crashing in the bushes, and the next minute a big red-skin come rushing at me with his tomahawk in his hand. I cocked my rifle, and kept my eye on him, ready to let him have my ball as soon as he should come close enough. He saw this, however, and he darted behind two good-sized saplings, which were about a foot apart. Neither of these trees was big enough to cover him, and, to keep me from getting a shot at him, he kept jumping from one to the other; and for the life of me, I couldn't help laughing at him, he did it so comically.

"I knew I had two of the varmints to deal with, and so I kept a pretty sharp lookout for the other. I saw him, at last, behind a tree, loading his gun. The tree wasn't quite big enough to cover him, and I found that I stood a better chance of hitting him than the other one; so I let the other fellow keep up his dancing, and watched this one closely. As he was ramming his bullet down, he turned his side to me, and exposed himself fairly. I blazed away, and broke his hip, which brought him to the ground too much disabled to cause me any more trouble.

"The big Injun now stopped his dancing, as he knew that my gun was empty, and made a dash at me with his tomahawk raised. He stopped, about fifteen feet from me, and threw the tomahawk at me with all his strength. If he had hit me, I wouldn't have been here to-night; but I had my eye on him, and I dodged the blow, and the weapon flew far out of the reach of either of us. I then clubbed my rifle, and sprang at the fellow.

He was much bigger than me, but I rather think I had the advantage of him in muscle. I tried to knock him down with the but-end of my gun, but he jumped into a lot of saplings, and every time I'd strike at him, he'd dodge. In this way I broke the stock off my gun, and at last had nothing left but the naked barrel. I could have easily killed him with this, if I could have got a fair lick at him; and at last, thinking I had a fair chance, I swung the iron at him, in a side lick, with such force that the thing flew clean out of my hands, entirely beyond my reach. The big Injun gave a yell at this, and sprang at me. Neither of us had a weapon of any kind, and I saw that we were in for a rough roll-and-tumble fight. I was always pretty good at this, and I closed with him at once, and down he went like a log. I couldn't hold him down, though, for as he was naked, and had his hide oiled, he could easily slip out of my grasp, and get up on his feet agin'. I threw him down five or six times, but found it impossible to hold him down. My wind was gitting pretty short, and I found that I must end the matter pretty soon; so I resolved to change my plan. I threw the Injun down agin', but, without trying to hold him, jumped on my feet, and as the fellow got up, I hit him a crack between the eyes with my fist, that sent him sprawling on his back. This astonished him, I can tell you; but he was up and at me in a second, when I hit him another crack, and knocked him down agin'. He got up slower this time, and I sent him down a third time. I did this about half a dozen times, and every time he got up slower. At last I had a fair chance, and I let fly at him, striking him just back of the ear. He went down about a little more than half stunned, and I jumped on him, and, clutching his throat with my left hand, tried to choke him to death, keeping my right hand free for use, if I should need it. The fellow wasn't so dead as I thought, though, for in a minute I felt him moving his right arm, which lay across my body, and looking down I saw that he was trying to git at his hunting-knife, which was hanging at his belt. The knife was very short, and was so tightly wedged in the sheath that the fellow had to git it out by pressing his finger against the point. I kept my eye on him, and let him work the handle out, and then, reaching over suddenly, I grabbed it, drew it from the sheath, and drove it with all my force into his heart. He gave a groan, and straightened himself out as dead as a hammer.

"I knew I had disabled the other Indian, but to what extent I couldn't say, and it was just as likely as not that he might shoot me at any moment; so I sprang to my feet, and commenced to look after him. I found that the varmint had crawled some distance towards the place where I'd been fightin' his pardner, and that he had propped his back agin' a log, and was tryin' to bring his gun to bear on me. Every time he tried to aim it, however, he would fall forward, and would have to push agin' his gun to raise himself. I didn't feel like bein' shot by a crippled Injun, and I thought I'd had about as much exercise as was good for me; so I started off as fast as I could for the block-house. I got there about nightfall; and a hard-looking case I was, too. I had no cap, no hunting-shirt, no horse, and no gun; and the worst of it was, that the folks in the fort didn't believe the story I told 'em. So I did just what you did, John, when I didn't believe the story you told of your escape; I told 'em I'd go with 'em and show 'em the place.

"The next day we started out, — about half a dozen in all, — and when we came to the place where I'd had the fight, I began to feel pretty mean. Thar lay the dead horse, but not a sign of a dead Injun was to be seen. The men commenced to laugh at me then, and I felt like a fool. We looked about, however, and found a trail, as if something had been dragged away. We followed it, and in about five minutes found the body of the big

Injun lying beside a log, covered up with leaves. The trail continued for a few hundred yards further, and thar we found the Injun I had crippled lying on his back, with his own hunting-knife sticking up to the hilt in his body, just below the breast-bone. It was plain that he had killed himself, finding that his wound had rendered it impossible for him to go any further. We had a long search for the knife with which I killed the big Injun, but at last we found it. The crippled Injun had forced it down into the ground by the weight of his heel.

"It was my turn to laugh now, as I had proved to my companions the truth of my story; but I couldn't do it, for the life of me. The way that crippled Injun had stood by his friend, even after he was almost gone himself, touched my heart, and I couldn't help feelin' sorry for the fellow. He was a brave man and a true friend, if he was an Injun, and I have always respected his memory ever since; for 'tain't often you find such true fellows among the red-skins. They're generally pretty apt to shift for themselves in times of trouble. That was about the toughest tussle I ever had with the varmints, and I haven't the least desire for another like it. But, hallo!" he exclaimed, starting to his feet, as a bright, red light shone in through the loop-holes, "what are they up to now?"

All rushed to the loop-holes and looked out. The bright glare of a fire lit up the fields and woods, and the settlers saw that the savages had fired the stack of fodder in the corn-field. It was a lucky thing for them that so little was left exposed to the enemy, for the whole crop would have shared the same fate had it been left without the walls of the fort. The Indians kept well under the cover of the woods, however, and not one of them could be seen. The fire burned down at length, and during the hours of darkness the embers continued to glow dimly. The night passed away quietly, and towards morning all but the sentinels were permitted to go to sleep; and in consequence of this, it was some time after sunrise before the garrison was stirring again.

The Indians had carried off their wounded and slain comrades, under the cover of the darkness, and they took good care not to add to their list of casualties by exposing themselves again. They hung about the fort during the day and a part of the next, firing an occasional shot on the morning of the third day, but at length abandoned their enterprise, and withdrew in the direction of the Ohio.

CHAPTER IX.

THE SCOUT.

By the spring of 1777 the country along the Ohio River, on the Virginia side, was beginning to be very well settled. There was a chain of forts, or block-houses, extending from Buffalo Creek, where the town of Wellsburg now stands, to below Fish Creek. Of these, the most important were Rice's Fort, on Buffalo Creek, about twelve or fifteen miles from its mouth, the fort at Wheeling (the name of which was now changed from Fort Fincastle to Fort Henry, in honor of Patrick Henry, the great champion of American liberty), and the fort at Grove Creek. That at Fish Creek was comparatively isolated, and had not yet acquired the importance which the others had attained. The country from the Ohio River towards the Monongehela was more thickly settled, and was growing stronger every day; but that portion lying immediately along the former stream was still weak, and exposed to the savages.

In the spring of 1777, however, a number of clearings were made back of Fish Creek. Captain Oxenford and the commanding officer at Grove Creek warned the parties making these settlements of the danger they were incurring in separating themselves from the communities already established; but the new comers, trusting more in their own judgment than in the experience of those who had preceded them, replied that they did not apprehend any danger, and that they could easily take refuge in one of the forts in case the Indians did make a descent upon them. It was impossible to compel these people to listen to reason, and they were left to themselves. As we shall see, the sequel proved the wisdom of the older settlers. During the spring several men came into the fort to seek shelter. They were all experienced woodsmen, and Captain Oxenford was glad to receive them, as they formed a very valuable addition to the garrison.

In spite of the danger which attended it, the regular work of putting in the crops was done. In order to guard against a surprise, scouts were thrown out at a distance of an eighth of a mile beyond the cornfield, and once or twice they exchanged shots with a straggling Indian lurking near; but, with these exceptions, the savages left the settlement in peace during the spring.

About the second week in July, however, the sentinel on duty at the gate of the Fish Creek fort saw a man and a woman running from out the woods towards the fort. The woman had something clasped in her arms, and the man carried a good-sized child in his. As they came near, the sentinel saw that they were whites, and that the bundle in the woman's arms was an infant. The gate was thrown open, and the fugitives rushed in. They were at once surrounded by the settlers, who recognized them as a family which had recently located in a clearing about six miles from the fort. When they were sufficiently recovered, they said, in reply to the questions of the settlers, that they had been awakened a little before daybreak by a succession of yells, which they knew at once could come only from Indians. Springing from their bed, they rushed to the door and looked out. Two cabins, which stood at a distance of a quarter of a mile from them, were in flames, and the Indians were yelling and dancing like fiends about the burning buildings. There could be no doubt as to the fate of the occupants of the cabins, and it was certain that the savages would visit the cabin of the Jones family, — for this was the name of the fugitives, — in a few minutes. There was no time to be lost, if they would save their lives; and so, catching up their children from the bed, they left the cabin, and, hurrying into the woods, fled towards the fort. They had not gone far when they heard a yell of rage in the direction of their house, and immediately a bright glare shot up above the trees, and they knew their home was in flames. They hastened on, however, with all their speed, and reached the fort almost exhausted with fatigue. It was still early morning when they arrived, and the day was bright and clear. A thin smoke hovering above the woods in the direction of the clearing of the Joneses confirmed their story.

Every one felt that the misfortunes of the fugitives, who had now lost everything in the world, was due to their folly in refusing to come into the fort when warned by Captain Oxenford; but this did not prevent the settlers from according them their warmest sympathy. A cabin in the fort was assigned them, and each family gave them something from their little store, so that by nightfall the Joneses were tolerably comfortable. They had a cabin to themselves, an abundance of food, and a bed for themselves and the children.

The next day, no signs of the Indians having been seen about the fort, Captain Oxenford proposed that a party should go out and ascertain the fate of the people who had been attacked by the savages. As the enemy might still be lurking in the neighborhood, this mission would be attended with some danger, and he called for volunteers to accompany him. Seven men volunteered to go with him, and at their earnest request, John and Dan were allowed to join the party. Tom Jones was one of the number, and he was directed to act as guide. The arms of the men were carefully examined before starting, and at eight o'clock the party left the fort for the scene of the massacre. They travelled rapidly, but cautiously, and reached the place in about two hours after setting out. Nothing was seen or heard of the savages on the way, and it was supposed that they had withdrawn from the vicinity immediately after the attack on the cabins.

Upon reaching the site of Jones's cabin, which was the first on the route, they found it in ashes. Everything was destroyed. The growing corn was trampled down, and the carcasses of his cow, pigs, and sheep lay near the site of the cabin. The savages had evidently taken great pains to make their work of destruction as complete as possible, and the owner of the clearing had been unusually fortunate in escaping with his family in safety. The ground, which was soft clay, bore the marks of many feet, and upon a careful examination of this trail, Bill Davis, the hunter, said that the enemy had numbered about fifteen men. Following the trail, the settlers came to the ruins of the two cabins which had been first assailed. The work of destruction was as complete here as at the cabin of the Joneses. All the buildings were in ashes, the stock lay about, with their throats cut, and the corn was trampled down and destroyed. But this was not the worst. A heap of charred bones in the midst of the ashes told that the occupants of the dwelling had either fallen by the hands of the enemy, and had been flung into the flames, or that they had been burned to death. One of the families had consisted of six people, three of whom were young children, and the other of four, namely, the parents and two half-grown girls. Six of them had perished on the spot, but the other four had evidently been carried into captivity, for there were the marks of shoes on the ground, one of them a girl's, another a man's, another a woman's, and the fourth print was made by the bare feet of a little child. The men followed the trail for some distance, and found that it led towards the Ohio, at a point above the mouth of Fish Creek. The savages had evidently escaped with their prisoners, so that it was useless to think of following them. The men then went back to the clearing, and collecting the blackened bones, buried them in a common grave, which they dug with their hunting-knives. This done, they returned to the fort, which they reached late in the afternoon.

Several weeks passed away without any further trouble from the savages. Towards the middle of August, Captain Oxenford was accosted one morning by Bill Davis, the hunter, as he was crossing the yard of the fort. The old man had just returned from a visit to Wheeling, and had been waiting for an hour or two to see the captain.

"I say, cap'," he said, as the commander of the fort passed him, "I want to speak a word with you."

"Well," said the captain, pausing, "what is it?"

"I saw Colonel Shepherd at Fort Henry yesterday," said the hunter, in a low tone, "and he told me to say to you that a lot of muskets and ammunition had been sent there from the east, for the forts along the border. You'll get your share to-morrow. They'll be put on a raft at Wheeling to-night, and floated down the Ohio to the mouth of this here creek. They'll be here by daybreak, and you must have your men there to receive them. The colonel says you must be very cautious, as a number of Indian scouts have been seen in this part of the country."

The men were ordered to hold themselves in readiness a little before daybreak the next morning, and at that time they set off for the mouth of the creek, taking with them two or three of the horses. A force was left at the fort, sufficient to hold it against any attack, but no one was informed of the object of the expedition. They reached the mouth of the creek about daylight. The raft was in sight, floating slowly down the current. The river was very low at this season, and the current was sluggish. It was half an hour before the vessel reached the place where the party had halted. It brought two men from the garrison of Fort Henry, and two boxes, containing twenty muskets, several kegs of powder, and a quantity of bullets. As the raft touched the shore, two or three rifle-shots were fired from the Indian side, showing that the enemy were not far away, and that the precautions of Colonel Shepherd were necessary. It was but the work of a few minutes to remove the articles from the raft, and transfer them to the pack-saddles with which the horses were provided. This done, the party returned to the fort, covering their march with a detachment, consisting of Bill Davis, and two other men, who remained half an hour on the river shore, to observe the movements of the enemy. The Indians made no effort to come over the stream, however, and the hunter came to the conclusion that the force on the opposite shore was merely a party of scouts, from whom they need not fear an attack.

The arms and ammunition were sent out by the government of the State of Virginia, and were to be used only for the defence of the fort. They were carefully put away in the store-house. The settlers were all provided with rifles, which they preferred to muskets, and they declared they had but little confidence in the efficacy of the heavy smooth-bores.

Several days after this the old hunter announced his intention of making a scout in the Indian country. Seeking out John Oxenford, who was now a well-grown youth of eighteen, he asked him if he would like to accompany him. John replied that nothing would please him better, provided his father's consent to the undertaking could be obtained; and this the hunter undertook to gain. He at once sought the captain, and laid his request before him. Captain Oxenford was willing that his sons — for Thomas was now a boy large enough for such things — should bear their part of the dangers and trials to which the whole settlement was subject; but he hesitated at the thought of allowing John to encounter the perils of the proposed expedition, for which there was really no necessity.

"He's got to learn to be an Injun-fighter, pretty soon, cap'," said the hunter, "and he had just as well begin now; and, though I say it, he won't find a better teacher anywhere than me."

"I know that, Davis," said the captain. "There isn't a man in the settlement that I'd trust quicker than you; but I don't see the use of this scout. It seems to me like flying in the face of danger."

"Not a bit of it," said the hunter. "I should die with the blues if I didn't take one of these tramps occasionally. You'd better let the boy go with me. It'll do him good."

The captain hesitated a long time, but, at length, yielded to the argument, that, as John had to begin his education as an "Injun-fighter" before very long, he might as well commence at once. He consented, however, upon the condition that the hunter should return in a fortnight, to which the old man agreed. John then donned his best suit of deer-skin and his bear-skin cap, and took the rifle which he had won from the Indian he had killed at the time of his escape, and set out with the old man.

They left the fort at sunset one bright August afternoon, and, as they turned into the woods, they paused to wave *adieu* to the boy's parents, who were standing at the gate, watching them depart. They were soon out of sight of the fort, however, and John was glad of it, for his eyes filled with tears as he looked back at those he loved so much.

"Never mind, lad," said the hunter; "we'll be back before long, and I'll warrant me you'll have a rare story to tell the old folks."

They passed along leisurely, and, a little after dark, reached the Ohio, about half way between the mouths of Grove Creek and Fish Creek. The river was so low that the water in the channel came only to their waists, and, removing their moccasons and leggings, they passed over to the Indian shore without difficulty. Once in the country of the savages, the hunter's manner changed. His footsteps were lighter and more cautious, and he was constantly on the alert. At the slightest sound he would pause and listen intently. He spoke very little; and when he did so, it was in the lowest and most cautious tone. They struck off boldly from the Ohio; and by the moonlight John could see that they were following a beaten track, which his companion informed him was a Shawnee trail. They camped for the night in the thick woods, just as the moon went down, and were up the next morning by sunrise. They breakfasted on the provisions they had brought with them, and which consisted of dried venison and parched corn.

During the day they travelled silently, — that is, very rarely indulging in conversation, — and two more days were passed in the same way. On the morning of the fourth day the hunter shot a stag, as the animal was drinking at a brook, a little after sunrise. They cut off such meat as they could use, and dragged the carcass into the trees. Then, building a fire by the side of the brook, they broiled the venison on the coals. The fatigue of the journey, and the light diet upon which they had been living, had, no doubt, sharpened the boy's appetite, for John thought he had never eaten anything so delicious as the rich venison steak which he helped to devour that morning.

Thus far they had seen nothing but game, at which Bill Davis would not allow his companion to fire, however, lest the report might draw the savages upon them, if any were lurking in the neighborhood. John asked him where the path they were following led. The hunter replied that it was the path to the Indian towns on the Scioto River, near which the present city of Chillicothe is located. He said he was going as near to those towns as he thought it prudent to venture, as he was anxious to see for himself if the Indians really meditated anything like an organized expedition against the whites. The old man now became more talkative than he had been, and told the boy many a story of his adventures among the savages. This day passed away very pleasantly in this manner, and at nightfall they went into camp again. They lighted no fire this time, as the hunter said they were too far in the Indian country to do so with prudence. About an hour after dark, Davis sprang to his feet with a sudden exclamation.

"What is the matter?" asked John, eagerly.

"Matter enough," replied Davis. "We are nearer to the Indians than I supposed."

"How do you know that?"

"I can see their camp fire," was the reply.

"I can see nothing," said John, looking around searchingly.

"That's likely enough, lad," said the hunter;

"but when you're as old as I am, and have had as much experience with the Injuns as I have, your eyes 'll be better. Look yonder."

The hunter pointed in the direction in which they had been travelling during the day, and John strained his eyes to see what had caused his alarm; but he was disappointed.

"I can see nothing," he said; "I think you must be mistaken."

The hunter laughed softly, and then, stepping behind the boy, he took his head between his hands, and turned his face in the direction in which he wished him to look.

"Now look at the tops of them hickory trees over yonder," he said. "Do you see a light haze just over the topmost branches?"

"Yes," answered John, after a pause, during which he made out the light distinctly, "I can see it very plainly."

"That," said the hunter, releasing his head, "is the glare of their camp fire on the sky. They are right in our track, and it's lucky we didn't build a fire to-night, for that might have betrayed us to them."

"Do you think there are many of them?" asked the boy.

"I can't say," answered the hunter. "The light isn't very strong on the sky, and I think they have only one fire, or two at the most, burning; but how many of them are in the gang is more than I can tell yet."

"What do you intend doing?" asked John.

"Well," said the hunter, slowly, "I'm going to take a peep at them."

"Then I'll go with you," said the boy. "It 'll be rare fun to see them without being seen."

"Well, lad, that depends upon circumstances. I've looked at Injuns at times when I thought it anything but fun. We've got into a very dangerous situation, and we might as well go forward as go back, for these red devils will find our trail in the morning, and pursue us. My plan is, to try and scare 'em off, if they are not too strong, and if they are, to go around them, and when they pass on in the morning, to fall in behind them, and travel in their rear. We'll have to be mighty cautious; and as you value your neck, my boy, you must obey every order I give, without waiting to have it explained."

"Very good," said John. "You will find me very obedient in all things."

"All right, then," said Davis. "Take your gun now, and come along. Put your feet down flat, so," he added, showing the boy how to place his feet, "and you'll make no noise. Now let's be off; and don't you talk, unless you are spoken to."

They set off slowly and cautiously, moving in the shade of the trees. The light over the trees grew brighter, and soon they could see it shining through the woods. Long experience, added to an unusual keenness of vision, had given the hunter the power of discerning objects by night as distinctly as in the day; and he led the way, scanning the dim woods closely, with strained eyes. Every moment brought the two nearer to the Indian camp, and increased their danger of stumbling across some of the savage scouts or sentinels; but Providence favored them, and they succeeded in gaining the very outskirts of the camp without being discovered. Here they paused, and, lying down in the undergrowth, peered anxiously through the bushes at the scene before them.

A large fire had been built, and around it about a dozen Indians were seated. They were hideously decked out with war-paint and feathers, and were evidently prepared for a grand foray upon the settlements. They were talking merrily about something which John could not understand, and would frequently burst into shouts of exultant laughter. The hunter, who could speak the Shawnee dialect, understood them, and John heard him grind his teeth furiously.

"I'm going up closer to them, to try to frighten them off," he whispered to John. "Lie here perfectly still. Don't fire, unless you hear me do so."

He crept away softly, and, after considerable exertion, managed to pass into the camp, and to climb into a large tree, the branches of which were not more than sixty feet from the fire. As he settled himself noiselessly among the boughs, he thought, for the first time, how foolish he had been in thus exposing himself and his companion to danger; and, as he looked down upon the scene below, he could not help asking himself how they should get away. The least sound might betray them, and he knew, if they fell into the hands of those below, they could expect no mercy. He had been too dangerous to them to hope they would spare him. He listened carefully to the talk of the savages, and then decided upon his plan of action, which was as singular as it was successful. It was a plan which not ten men in ten thousand could have carried out. Among his many natural gifts was that of ventriloquism; and as this had often been of use to him in his expeditions as a hunter and a scout, he determined to make use of it now. He understood thoroughly the superstitious nature of the Indian, and he was about to trust entirely to it for his own safety and that of his companion.

Carefully surveying the scene below, he crawled out noiselessly among the thick branches of a limb of the tree which was nearest to the fire. Then, throwing his voice down among the blazing fagots, he startled the Indians by crying, in a loud voice, in the Shawnee tongue, —

"Warriors, why have you started on the war-path? You are marching to your death!"

The savages sprang to their feet in astonishment, and the hunter lay very still in the tree. Then began a confused jabber of tongues, and the dusky group gathered around the fire, pointing to it, and gesticulating energetically. The Indians were very badly frightened; but at length a circle was formed around the fire, and one, who was evidently the chief, stepped out alone, preparatory to addressing them. As he opened his lips to speak, the hunter threw his voice into the chief's mouth, and gave a prolonged howl. The savage started back in dismay, and then Davis, with a remarkable facility, changed the voice from one painted brave to another, causing them to utter noises like cats and dogs, and to give utterance to the most insulting speeches. The chief tried to speak again, but before he could do so, the hunter shouted out from the fire, in good Shawnee, to return home at once; that the curse of the Great Spirit was upon the expedition. Then he made such a buzzing about the ears of the chief, that the man gave a yell of fear, and, turning, fled, at full speed, into the depths of the forest. The remainder of the band hesitated, but a fresh imprecation from the ventriloquist decided them, and they fled in dismay.

As soon as they were fairly out of sight, the hunter swung himself down from the tree, and, hastening to where he had left John, who had witnessed the scene with the most complete bewilderment, touched the lad hurriedly.

"Get up at once, John," he said, hastily. "We must be off from here. Those fellows may come back, after their fright wears off, and we must get as much of a start as we can."

John was on his feet in an instant, and the two set off rapidly. They realized the danger in which they were placed, and travelled without speaking, until about two hours before daybreak. Then, leaving the Indian trail, they turned into the woods, and the hunter bade John lie down and get as much sleep as possible, as they must be off at sunrise. John gladly obeyed, for he was worn out with the extraordinary fatigue of the past day, and, throwing himself down, he was soon fast asleep. His companion aroused him shortly after sunrise, and they continued their march, or, rather, their flight, until nightfall, when, finding that they were not pursued, the hunter decided to camp for the night.

During the day John asked the old man the cause of the sudden terror and flight of the Indians. The hunter laughed heartily at the question, and then explained to the boy the wonderful gift with which he was blessed. He made John pledge his honor never to reveal the secret, for, he said, it would be of no use to him if it got out, for the Indians would be sure to hear it, and he could never deceive them again.

On the afternoon of the fourth day, they reached the Ohio at the place where they had crossed it eight days before, and by sunset they were safe on the Virginia shore. They stopped at the water's edge to put on their lower garments, which they had removed in crossing, and were chatting gayly, — for the hunter considered that they were now out of danger, — when they were startled by the sharp crack of a rifle on the Indian side. The ball cut a hole in John's bear-skin cap, and startled him not a little. The two caught up their clothing, and hurried up the bank, where they finished their dressing, watching the Indian shore closely in the mean time; but no one was visible there.

"It was some Indian scout, I reckon," said the hunter, "and it's powerful lucky for us that he didn't blaze away at us while we were on the other side."

A rustle in the bushes attracted John's attention at this moment. He had cocked his rifle, and was holding it in readiness for use in case any one should attempt to cross the river after them; and as he heard the rustle in the bushes, which had escaped the hunter's ear, he turned abruptly, and saw, to his astonishment, an Indian, not twenty yards from them, in the act of aiming his rifle at them. It was the work of an instant to bring his gun to his shoulder and fire. The shot was at random, but it was excellent, for the ball struck the savage full in the forehead, just as he was in the act of sighting his rifle, and laid him on the ground, a lifeless corpse.

"What are you shooting at?" exclaimed the hunter, sharply; for he had been so much occupied in watching the Indian shore that he had been unconscious of the danger which had threatened them.

"Look yonder," said John, pointing to the dead Indian.

"Whew!" muttered the old man, turning

pale in spite of himself at the thought of his narrow escape, "they are as thick as hornets. That was well done, though, lad. You'll make a good hunter, if you live long enough. Come, now, and I'll show you how to take his sculp."

Conquering his repugnance, John went with the hunter to the body, and in a moment severed the savage's scalp from his head. This he swung at his belt, in true hunter style, while the old man secured the Indian's rifle, which he said was too good a weapon to be lost.

"Now," said John, "I suppose we may as well go back to the fort."

"Yes," replied the hunter; "the sooner we git thar, the better for us. These Injuns is mighty thick about here, and I'm afeard some mischief's afoot."

They struck through the woods at a rapid pace, and reached the fort about nine o'clock. They were at once admitted, and warmly welcomed. The old hunter told the story of the flight of the Indians without revealing his secret, and professed to regard it as a very mysterious affair. While John wisely concluded to volunteer no information upon the subject, Bill Davis was loud in his praise of the boy for his conduct during the scout, and the manner in which he had killed the Indian drew forth the old man's warmest admiration.

CHAPTER X.

THE SIEGE.

THE next morning Bill Davis was up at sunrise as fresh as ever; but John slept late, as he was unused to such severe fatigue as he had undergone during the scout, and was stiff and sore from it. As the hunter crossed the yard, he saw Tom Oxenford, now a little over sixteen years old, and a good-sized boy, standing near the gate, fixing his gun hastily.

"What's the matter, Tom?" he asked, attracted by the eagerness with which the boy was working. "What are you doing that for?"

"I'm going to shoot a turkey that I hear gobbling on the hill-side," replied the boy.

"I hear no turkey," said the hunter, listening.

"I heard him distinctly just a minute ago,"

said Tom, "and if he's there yet, I mean to have him. There, don't you hear him?" he exclaimed.

This time the hunter did hear what the boy supposed to be a turkey, and in a few minutes the sound was repeated again.

"Well, Tom," said the old man, quietly, "I'll go and kill that turkey."

"No, you won't," cried Tom; "it's my turkey, for I heard it first."

"Your father's orders are positive that you shall not leave the fort," said the hunter. "Besides, I'm the best marksman; and as I don't want the turkey, I'll go and kill it for you."

Tom had forgotten all about his father's orders in his eagerness to get a shot at the turkey, and he recollected now that it would be impossible for him to leave the fort in the face of this prohibition. He handed his gun to the hunter with a sigh.

"All right, Bill," he said; "but remember it's my turkey."

Bill Davis left the fort at once; but instead of going in the direction of the sound, he walked rapidly up the creek, to the disappointment of Tom, who felt sure that he would miss the turkey. The hunter entered the woods about a quarter of a mile above the fort, and, guided by the gobbling, passed around through the trees, in order to come upon the turkey from behind. In a few minutes he came in sight of it, and a glance confirmed his suspicions. An Indian was sitting on a chestnut stump, partially concealed by a small bush, and was gobbling like a turkey. He was waitirg to see if any one would come out from the fort to kill the turkey, in which case he would be sure to kill the person before the latter could discover the deception. He was utterly unconscious of the hunter's presence, however, and the old man crept up cautiously within easy range of him, and shot him through the head. He took the fellow's scalp, and hastened back to the fort.

Tom Oxenford, who had been waiting

impatiently at the fort, heard the shot, and was in great eagerness to get his prize. As he saw the old man come in through the gateway without the turkey, he almost cried with vexation.

"There, now," he exclaimed, sharply, "you've let the turkey go. I knew you would. I would have killed it if I had gone."

"I didn't let it go, Tom," said the hunter, quietly.

"Then where is it?" asked the boy.

"There," replied the old man, throwing the bloody scalp down on the ground before the boy. "There, Tom, take your turkey; I don't want it."

Tom gazed at the scalp in utter bewilderment, and then there flashed across his mind a full sense of the dreadful fate from which Bill Davis's quickness and good sense had saved him; and seizing the old man's hand, he burst into tears.

"There, there, lad," said the hunter, laughing; "don't blubber at a dead Injun's sculp.

But I say, Tom," he added, roguishly, "don't you ever mistake a red-skin for a turkey agin'."

The incident was soon known throughout the fort, and "Tom's turkey" became a by-word.

A week passed away quietly. About the tenth of September, news was received from Grove Creek that the savages, under the infamous renegade Simon Girty, had attempted to capture Fort Henry, at Wheeling, and had been defeated. The messenger went back to Grove Creek that night, and as it was not improbable that the Indians might make an attempt on the fort at Fish Creek, Captain Oxenford resolved to be on his guard.

Four of the men left the fort one morning to cross over to the south side of the creek to get a kettle that had been left in one of the cabins. They had reached the water, and were about to ford it, when several shots were fired at them from the woods. One of the men fell dead at the verge of the creek, and the other three started at full speed for the fort. The gate was held in readiness to admit them; but as they came within fifty yards of the defences, a heavy volley was poured at them from the woods with fatal effect.

"Bar up the gate, boys," cried Bill Davis, quickly. "Them poor fellows is out of harm's way now; but, if I ain't mightily mistaken we're in for a sight of work."

The gate was made fast, and the settlers, alarmed by the heavy firing, came rushing out of their cabins into the yard, to learn the cause of it. The first person that approached Bill Davis was the wife of one of the men who had been killed. The hunter did not know how to tell her of her loss, and he ran by her without replying to her eager questions.

"Get your guns, men," he shouted; "the fort is attacked."

Then hurrying to Captain Oxenford's quarters, he called to Mrs. Oxenford, who was busy helping her husband to cut away the wooden strips which covered the loop-holes.

"Mrs. Oxenford," said he, "Vent and Spencer have been killed by the savages. Please go and tell their wives, for I haven't the heart to do it. You women can do these things better than I can."

Mrs. Oxenford hastened to the cabins of the afflicted families, but the poor women had already heard the sad news, and were weeping violently. She did what she could to comfort them; but, ah! the kindest, tenderest sympathy is powerless to console in cases like this.

"How many men have we lost, Davis?" asked Captain Oxenford, as his wife went out.

"Four, sir; Vent and Spencer, and two of the hunters. Vent was killed first, and the others were cut down by that volley you heard jist now. Take my word for it, cap', we've got trouble in store for us, for thar's a strong body of Injuns in them woods."

Captain Oxenford, having cleared away the loop-holes in his quarters, now hurried into the yard of the fort, and summoned the men to his side. The garrison at this time consisted of sixteen able-bodied men and boys, all of whom were good marksmen. These were required to have their powder-horns and bullet-pouches slung at their sides, and the women were set to moulding the lead into bullets, and preparing bandages for those who might be wounded. These things once arranged, the men were ordered to occupy the cabins and block-houses on the side nearest the Indians, who were still in the woods.

It was but seven o'clock in the morning, and the day was bright and beautiful. The Indians were still concealed in the woods, and had remained perfectly quiet after firing the volley which killed the settlers, not even venturing out to scalp their victims. Half an hour passed away, and the silence began to be oppressive. The garrison had orders to await the movements of the enemy, and to fire slowly and deliberately, and not to waste a shot. At the end of the half hour a terrific yell arose from the woods, and the Indians emerged from their cover, and advanced towards the fort. They were about three hundred strong, and their line extended from the woods around to the creek, and down to the cornfield in the bottom. As they left the woods, a loud whoop arose on their right, and was taken up and passed along their line from right to left. They threw their left wing into the cornfield, their right clung to the woods just back of the fort, and detached parties were thrown into the cabins and stables of Captain Oxenford and Mr. Whittaker, which were within rifle range of the fort. This disposition of the savage forces was very skilful, as it placed nearly every man under cover, and occupied ground from which a sharp fire could be directed upon the fort. It took about twenty minutes to complete these arrangements, and at the end of that time an Indian advanced from the woods towards the fort, carrying a dirty white cloth, which he waved as a flag of truce. He paused within speaking distance, and gave a loud halloo!

"What do you want?" asked Captain Oxenford, who was standing at one of the loop-holes.

"Me big Injun — heap," said the savage, striking his breast pompously.

"You are very well grown for your age, my beauty," cried Bill Davis, who was looking out from the loop-hole next to the captain.

The settlers greeted this remark with a laugh, which seemed to excite the Indian's wrath, for he struck his breast still more violently, and called out lustily, —

"Me big Injun; much heap."

"What do you want?" called Captain Oxenford again.

"Give up, give up fort," shouted the savage. "Too many Injun. Injun too big. No kill."

"You are a parcel of cowards," cried the captain. "Come on as soon as you wish. We are ready for you; and as soon as you show your yellow hides, we'll make holes in them for you."

"Go back," called the old hunter, mockingly. "Tell your people to send a warrior to talk with us. You are an old squaw."

The savage uttered a howl of rage as he heard the insulting language of the hunter. He shook his fist at the walls, and called out something in the Indian tongue. Just then Tom Oxenford, unable to resist the temptation, fired at him, and the ball struck him in the arm, causing him to drop his flag, and take to his heels.

As the wounded red-skin reached his lines, the Indians fired a general volley at the fort, and the very earth seemed to shake under the discharge of the three hundred rifles. The settlers could hear the balls strike the logs with a dull thud; but as all the whites were under cover, no one was hurt. The firing was now kept up pretty rapidly, the savages feeling so sure of success that they fired at random. The principal attack was upon the north side of the fort, and the main strength of the garrison was collected there, only one of the boys being stationed in each of the other block-houses to fire upon the enemy, and watch their movements in that quarter. The whites fired slowly and deliberately, and whenever a dusky warrior exposed himself at all, he was sure to receive a rifle-ball as the reward of his daring. The savages acted in a very reckless manner, and it was evident that they were all very much under the influence of whiskey. Late in the afternoon the enemy advanced closer to the fort on the side of the woods, and as, in doing so, they exposed themselves more than they had previously done, the fire from the fort became more rapid and fatal.

John Oxenford had been stationed in the block-house overlooking the cornfield, to which the Indian left wing still clung. He could only see an occasional puff of smoke from the rows of corn, and hear the crack of a hostile rifle immediately afterwards, but during the morning he could not get a shot at anything. The firing on the other side of the fort excited him very much, and it required all his resolution to enable him to stay at his post.

In the afternoon, however, matters changed. The Indians, finding that their fire was not returned on this side of the fort, seemed to think that the attention of the garrison was occupied on the other side, and that they might be able to send a party over the walls in this quarter. About four o'clock Dan Whittaker came into the block-house, where John was standing, looking eagerly through a loop-hole at the movements of the Indians.

"John," he said, "your father has sent me here to ask how matters are going in this quarter. What shall I say?"

"I haven't had a shot at them to-day, Dan," said John, without turning his head.

"What are you looking at?" asked Dan, going to one of the loop-holes.

"Look at those Indians in the cornfield," said John. "What are they doing?"

"They seem to be coming this way," said Dan. "You keep an eye on 'em, John, and I'll go ask the captain to send some of the men to this side."

Dan ran out of the block-house, and hastened across the yard.

"I'll have a shot this time," thought John; and sure enough he was right.

About thirty Indians now left their cover in the cornfield, and commenced to creep stealthily towards the fort. Their rifles were slung across their backs, and they were unencumbered with anything that could impede their progress. John watched them eagerly, and, cocking his rifle, brought it up to the loophole. The next moment the Indians were within a hundred yards of the walls. One of them, who seemed to be the leader of the party, raised his hand above his head, to wave on his men; and, taking advantage of this, John drew a bead on his exposed breast, and fired. The savage tottered for an instant, and then fell heavily to the ground. At this moment Dan Whittaker and one of the hunters came bounding into the room.

"They're right on us, Dan. Be quick," cried John, who was reloading his rifle with all possible speed.

"All right," said Dan, as his companion and himself took their posts at the loop-holes. "There are three more men in the block-house at the other corner."

The Indians had hesitated for a moment, as they saw their leader fall; but they dashed forward now at a sharp run, encouraged by the fact that but one shot had been fired at them. They were doomed to disappointment, however, for the five men, who had come to John's assistance, opened on them from the two corners of the fort which commanded their approach, and as each man had marked out his victim, the fire resulted in the death of five Indians. Still the savages pressed on, uttering yells that made the hearers' blood run cold. They reached the base of the walls, and some of them tried to climb up the smooth sides to the roof above; but the defenders had now reloaded, and were prepared for them. Each one fired at will; and, as the savages were within point-blank range, the shots were all effective. Not one was thrown away. Two of the red-skins were shot on the walls, and the savages began to find that they were in a very warm place; so, abandoning the undertaking, they fled in dismay to the cornfield, leaving nine of their men on the ground, and carrying off four or five wounded. The settlers were all tried marksmen, and it was very rare that their shots resulted in anything but death.

"That was pretty well done," said Dan Whittaker, as the Indians disappeared in the standing corn. "I don't think they'll try that again very soon."

"I reckon not," said John. "They've been very severely punished; but it was lucky for us all, Dan, that you came here when you did. I couldn't have given the alarm and watched those fellows at the same time; and it was my shooting that chief that made the red-skins halt. If they had kept on, they might have climbed the wall before you and the others came."

Late in the afternoon a sharp fire, accompanied by loud yells, was opened on the west side of the fort, which drew most of the garrison in that direction. Under the cover of this attack, a party of eighteen or twenty Indians, armed with rails and logs of wood, made an impetuous dash at the gateway of the fort. The movement was detected, however, by old Bill Davis.

"Come on, boys," he cried, excitedly, rushing to the cabins where the men were engaged; "the red devils are beating down the gate. Quick! they'll be inside in a minute."

Captain Oxenford sent ten men, with the old man, to the row of stables, the loop-holes of which commanded the gateway. They arrived in good time, for the savages were already battering away at the enclosure, which was not capable of withstanding such heavy blows. The settlers opened a sharp fire upon the astonished Indians, who had imagined that their movement was not known to the whites, and in five minutes the enemy were driven back, with the loss of five or six of their number. Their comrades greeted this failure with yells of rage, and until sunset poured a heavy fire upon the fort from all sides. Only one man was wounded in the garrison. A rifle ball came into one of the block-houses, through a loop-hole, and struck one of the settlers in the shoulder. The wound was painful, but not at all dangerous, and the man was turned over to the women, who dressed his shoulder.

At nightfall the fire of the savages slackened, and for several hours only an occasional shot was fired. No one slept in the fort. The men were equally distributed among the four block-houses, and were ordered to hold themselves in readiness to repel an attack at any moment. There was no necessity for this order, however, for no one felt like sleeping with the enemy so near.

John Oxenford, Dan Whittaker, and Bill Davis were all in the same block-house. No lights were allowed in the fort, for it was feared that they might draw the fire of the savages upon the loop-holes, and that some one might be injured in this way. The two boys rarely left the loop-holes, and kept straining their eyes through the darkness to try to make out the movements of the enemy. About an hour after midnight, John touched Dan, and told him to watch the ground about half way between the two block-houses on this side of the fort.

"There is something moving there, I am certain," he said, in a low tone.

"Nonsense," said Dan; "it's your imagination."

"I mean to give it a shot, anyhow," said John; and, slipping his gun through the loop-hole, he aimed carefully at the object which had attracted his attention. The report of his rifle was answered by a howl of pain, and the boys heard the scampering of feet in the direction of the Indian lines.

"What do you think of that, Dan?" John asked, triumphantly.

"Well," replied Dan, "you were right it seems; but I never should have fired at that thing."

The next morning it was found that the Indians had removed their dead during the night, and had scalped and horribly mutilated the settlers that had been killed at the opening of the attack. On the spot where John had wounded the Indian during the night was a considerable quantity of fodder and dried grass. The boy pointed it out to the old hunter, and asked if he could tell why it was placed there.

"O, yes," replied the old man; "that's plain enough. The varmint you shot last night was tryin' to put it under the wall of the fort."

"What was that for?" asked the boy.

"To burn us out, you ninny," said the old man, laughing; "but when you hit him, he dropped it, I suppose, and ran back; so your shot saved us a powerful sight of trouble. Putting out that fire under the rifles of the red-bellies wouldn't have been any fun, I can tell you."

The savages reopened the attack at sunrise, and continued it during the day. Their losses had been so severe, however, that they were more prudent than during the first day. They kept under cover, and it was rare that the settlers were able to inflict any injury upon them. The men were much worn down by loss of sleep and fatigue, and Captain Oxenford, thinking it likely that it would be necessary to keep them up all night, stationed a sentinel in each block-house, with orders to keep up a show of firing, and gave the rest permission to sleep on the floor of the block-houses in which they were stationed. He did not close his eyes, however.

During all this time, the women had behaved nobly. Even the poor creatures whose husbands had been killed kept their grief to themselves, and refrained from embarrassing or unmanning the defenders of the fort by a show of timidity. They were busy moulding bullets, and kept the men well supplied with them. They served them with their meals at their posts, and throughout the whole siege not a murmur or a timid word was heard from them. They were a brave, heroic race, those pioneer women, and they were worthy mothers of the men who have made the sweet west so powerful and glorious.

Bill Davis kept the captain company. He could not sleep, he said, with the rifles of the enemy cracking all around him, and as for fatigue, he was used to that. He kept a close watch over the movements of the enemy, for he had very little faith in the vigilance of the sentinels in the block-houses.

"Look yonder, cap'," he exclaimed; "look at them Injuns by your cabin, over yonder. Hang me if they hain't got a white gal along with 'em."

The captain looked in the direction indicated, and, sure enough, there was a white woman in the midst of the savages. She disappeared in a few minutes, leaving the two men very much perplexed by her presence in such inappropriate company.

"She's a prisoner, I reckon," said the hunter. "She's some poor cretur the red-bellies has stolen away; and if they don't kill her, they'll take her with 'em, and make a squaw of her; and, to my mind, that's jist as bad as losin' your har."

At sunset the fire of the Indians was increased, and a fresh attempt was made to storm the gateway; but this was driven off, with a loss of six or seven men to the enemy.

As the savages retired, the defenders heard a loud cheer without, accompanied by rapid firing, and a succession of Indian yells. The sounds grew louder, and seemed to be coming towards the fort. The hunter hastened to the block-house, which commanded a view of the spot from which the noise proceeded. The next moment he came rushing back.

"Open the gate," he shouted. "There's a company of mounted men coming to help us, and they're cutting their way through the Injuns. Open the gate, and let 'em in."

The horsemen were now within a few yards of the fort, and, as the gate was thrown open, they dashed into the enclosure at full speed. The Indians pressed on hotly after them, and tried to enter the fort with them; but the settlers, who had been expecting this, gave the savages a volley which sent them reeling back towards the cornfield. The gate was closed and securely barred, and the garrison turned to welcome their friends. The new comers consisted of twenty men from Grove Creek. They had heard of the attack on the fort from their scouts, and had hastened to the assistance of their friends. Fortunately, they had but two men wounded in cutting their way through the Indians. They were warmly welcomed, for their generous heroism was fully appreciated by the settlers.

After the arrival of the horsemen, the fire of the Indians ceased altogether, and during the next five or six hours, everything was perfectly still. Some of the settlers thought the savages had given up the siege and withdrawn; but Bill Davis shook his head sagely, and declared they were only up to some "deviltry."

About midnight, John Oxenford was crossing the yard from his father's quarters to the block-house, to which he had been assigned, and, in doing so, he passed by the gate. He thought he heard a faint tapping at it, and paused to listen.

"Please let me in," cried a plaintive voice without. John listened again, and the cry was repeated.

"Who are you, and what do you want?" he asked, going up to the gate.

"Let me in; the Indians will kill me," cried the voice, loudly. Then it added, in a low tone, "Can you hear me if I speak very low?"

"Yes," replied John, lowering his own voice; "but what do you want?"

"I'm a girl," said the voice in a low tone. "The Indians took me prisoner yesterday morning. They have sent me here to get you to open the gate and let me in; but don't do it — don't do it. As soon as you open the gate for me, they will rush in, and murder the garrison. They will kill me if I fail, but I had better die than all of you."

"Where are the Indians?" asked the boy, touched by the girl's heroism.

"They are lying on the ground within a few yards of the gate," she answered, "and can hear you, if you speak very loud."

"Stay here till I come back," said John, "and keep your ear close to the gate, so you can hear me when I speak to you. I mean to try to save you, and I think I can do it."

The girl continued her cry, and John hastened to find his father and the old hunter, to whom he related the strange occurrence.

"She's a noble girl," said the captain, "and we must save her, if we can."

"She's the gal we saw this morning," said the hunter; "and, between us, I think we can save her."

The old man then stated to the captain a plan for the rescue of the girl, which was instantly approved. The three then hastened to the gate, where the girl was still uttering her cries.

"Are you there yet?" asked John, in a low tone.

"Yes," she answered, cautiously.

"Where are the Indians?"

"In the same place."

"Can they see you?"

"No, not plainly; it is too dark."

"Then listen to me," said John. "A rope will be lowered over the wall, about three feet from the right hand side of the gate, in a few minutes. Move yourself there cautiously, and feel along the wall till you find the rope. Tie the lower end of it to your waist, and catch it above your head with your hands. When you have done this, pull the rope gently with your hands, so that we may know when you are ready, and we will draw you up on the roof."

"O, thank you! thank you!" said the girl, eagerly. "God bless you for your kindness."

"Hush!" said John. "The Indians will hear you. Now go, for we shall lower the rope right away."

John joined his father and the hunter, who had climbed to the roof of the stables, and had dropped one end of a stout rope over the wall at the appointed place. In a minute or two they felt the rope being drawn gently once or twice, which was the signal that all was in readiness below. All three then seized the rope, and, the girl's light weight offering but a slight obstacle to their united efforts, they soon had her drawn up to the roof. The next moment she was by their side.

"Now," said the captain, "get down that ladder into the yard, quick. They may see us."

He had scarcely spoken, when several shots were fired at them from without, followed by a scattering volley, telling plainly that the Indians had discovered the rescue of the girl, and the failure of their own ruse. But the fire did no damage. The girl had reached the yard, and the others lay down flat on the sloping roof, and the balls whistled over them. As soon as the firing ceased, they swung themselves down into the yard, where the rescued captive was awaiting them.

"Now, John," said the captain, "you and

Davis must go back to your posts. I'll take this girl to your mother, and she shall look after her to-night."

The group then separated. Towards morning a bright light shone in through the loop-holes, and it was found that the Indians were setting fire to the cabins outside of the fort.

"That's a good sign," said the hunter.

"Why?" asked John.

"It means that they've given up the hope of taking the fort, and are going away," was the reply. "I think we shall git off pretty well, my lad."

The hunter was right. The savages made no further demonstration during the night, and at sunrise there were no signs of them visible. The garrison remained in the fort during the day, but the next morning a party was sent out to follow the trail of the enemy, and found that they had fled across the Ohio into their own country. The danger being over, the Grove Creek horsemen bade adieu to their friends, and returned home.

The fort had been gallantly held. The savages numbered three hundred chosen warriors, and they were exasperated by their failure to take Fort Henry at Wheeling, and Rice's Fort, on Buffalo Creek, and were resolved to destroy the Fish Creek settlement at all hazards. Their loss was never known accurately, as they carried off their killed and wounded; but it was confidently believed to be not less than sixty, of whom the greater number were killed. The loss of the settlers was insignificant. Besides the four men who had been killed at the opening of the siege, only one of their number had been wounded. The two wounded men belonging to the Grove Creek horsemen were not members of the garrison, and they came when the victory was practically won. The settlers had a right to feel proud, for the stand they had made had been in defence of the liberties of America, as well as for their own immediate protection. The attack was one of a series inaugurated and carried on by the British Governor Hamilton, of Detroit, and the savages had been supplied with arms and materials of war by the government of Great Britain, which had resolved to destroy the young Republic, if it could not reduce it to submission.

CHAPTER XI.

THE CAPTURE.

The morning after the burning of the cabins by the Indians, John went home to breakfast, the first meal the family had eaten since the siege began. He found the young girl that had been rescued the night before helping his mother about her household duties, and as she saw him enter, she came forward frankly, and offered him her hand. She was a fine specimen of the frontier maiden, and there was not a prettier girl along the whole border. She was about his own age; and the roses on her cheeks would have extorted the envy of many a city belle. John took her offered hand bashfully, and his color deepened as she thanked him for saving her from the Indians. He stammered out something about being very glad to serve her, and his confusion was increased as he saw his mother glancing at him with a smile, the meaning of which he read at once. The good dame saw through the simple boy in an instant, and she was not altogether sorry that he had lost his heart from the moment he laid eyes on the pretty stranger.

The maiden said her name was Annie Clarke, and that she was an orphan. She had been living with some distant relatives, who had recently located a few miles back of the Grove Creek Fort. They had not thought it worth while to seek refuge in the fort; and on the day before the attack on the Fish Creek settlement, the savages had made a descent on their clearing, and had massacred all the family but the young girl. They had brought her with them, intending to carry her to their towns, and marry her to one of their young men. Being baffled in all their attempts to take the Fish Creek Fort, they had sent her to act as a decoy, hoping to surprise the garrison in this way; but the heroic girl had resolved to put the whites on their guard, even at the cost of her own life. The result had not been in accordance with her expectations. She said she had no friends in the world now, and that she knew not what to do.

After breakfast that morning, Mrs. Oxenford had a long talk with the captain about the pretty stranger. She had taken a decided interest in her, and she was anxious to keep her with her, as one of the family. She mentioned that she thought John was disposed to fall in love with her. She was glad of this, as she wanted him to marry as soon as he could after he came of age; and if he fancied this girl, she (his mother) would have an opportunity of contributing to the formation of the character of her son's wife. She had a dread of her boy's marrying a stranger. So it was settled that Annie Clarke should remain in the family as one of them. Nothing was to be said about the matrimonial part of the affair, but the young people were to be left to take their own course. Annie was well pleased with the offer of a home, and accepted it gratefully; and as for

John, he was delighted with the arrangement.

Three years passed away. John was now of age, and had grown up into a tall, fine-looking young fellow. Annie had fulfilled her early promise, and had become a beautiful woman, and it was decided that she and John should be married the next year. The settlers had remained in the fort since the events describeed in the last chapter; for although nothing of such a momentous character had transpired during the interval, the Indians had shown too much activity to make it safe for any one to live outside the walls of the fortification. There had been neither deaths nor removals to decrease the population of the settlement; but, on the contrary, there had been several additions to the community in the shape of three or four plump pioneer babies. The old hunter, Bill Davis, had abandoned his roving life to a great extent, and had settled down at the fort. He said he meant to wait there until John and Annie were married, and then he would pass the rest of his davs with them, wherever they might go.

It was exactly three years from the day of the attack on the fort, and was now the middle of September, 1780. About eight o'clock in the morning, a heavy, black smoke was seen rising in the direction of Grove Creek. It was evident that it proceeded from some extraordinary cause, and the settlers were very much perplexed about it.

"I'm afraid the fort at Grove Creek is on fire," said Captain Oxenford to the old hunter.

"So am I, cap'," replied the old man. "No ordinary cabin would make a smoke like that."

"I think we ought to send out and see what is the matter," said the captain. "You know our friends there came promptly to our assistance when they thought we were in danger."

"You are right, cap'," said the hunter. "I'll go if I can get ten men to go with me."

"I'll go," said John and Dan in a breath. Several others professed their willingness to join the party, and the number was soon made up. They left the fort at once, well armed, and took the shortest route to Grove Creek. They marched rapidly, in Indian file, the hunter leading the way. They had passed over half the distance between the two forts, when the hunter suddenly gave the command to halt.

"Boys," said he, in a low tone, "I can't get rid of the idea that thar's Injuns about. Now, it won't do for us to run right into 'em without knowing it."

"How will you prevent it?" asked one of the men.

"Easy," replied the hunter. "One of us must go ahead a little distance, and if thar's any Injuns about, they'll be apt to fire at him first, and the rest of us can get out of the way, or be ready for 'em."

"That's all very good, except for the man that goes ahead," said the settler.

"I intend to be that man," said the hunter, quietly.

"We'd better draw straws for it," said one of the men.

"Certainly; that will be fair," was the general exclamation.

"No, boys," said the hunter, firmly; "I'm in command of this party, and I'll expose none of you to the danger of such a venture. I'll do the reconnoitring myself. If I'm killed, why, nobody 'll miss me. You've all got mothers, and wives, and sisters at the fort, while I've got nobody but this here boy;" and he laid his hand affectionately on John's shoulder.

"Thank you, Bill," said John, softly.

"Now, boys," resumed the hunter, "I'll go ahead, and do you follow me at about a hundred yards' distance. Be ready for action at a second's warning."

The men caught their rifles at a "ready," and they set off again, with the hunter about a hundred yards in front. They passed over another mile of the way without speaking, when suddenly the hunter paused, and waited for them to come up with him.

"What is the matter?" asked John.

"Look yonder," said the old man, pointing along the pathway they were travelling; "don't you see them Injun trinkets? Well, sure as we live, the red-bellies themselves ain't far away."

The path a few yards in advance of them was strewn with Indian trinkets and beads, and the men felt very confident that the hunter was right in his suspicions of the proximity of the savages.

"What shall we do?" asked one of the men.

"We'll quit this path, and cut around through the woods," said the hunter. "It isn't safe to keep this road any longer; so we'll wheel about at once."

They were standing in a narrow bridle-path, with the thick woods on each side of them. As the hunter spoke, a heavy volley was poured into them from each side of the road. Two of them fell dead, and a third was slightly wounded.

"Take to the trees, and run for it, boys," shouted the hunter. "They've got to load agin."

The survivors now set off at a rapid pace for the fort, with the savages in hot pursuit.

There were about twenty Indians in the attacking party, and this number was reduced by three or four, who fell beneath the unerring rifles of the whites in the running fight which ensued, and which was continued for several miles. At length there was a sharp crack of a rifle immediately behind John Oxenford, and the young man felt something sting the calf of his leg; and the next instant he sank to the ground, utterly unable to run another step. He knew he had been wounded, and he expected to be killed the next moment. To his utter astonishment, he saw Dan Whittaker stop by his side. The savages were close at hand, and he called to Dan to make his escape.

"I'll stay here with you, John," said the brave fellow, quietly. "I said I'd stick by you through thick and thin, and I'll do it."

"But, Dan," said John, "they'll kill you, and you can do me no good by staying here."

"A man can't die but once," said Dan, coolly; "and if that's got to be your fate, I'll share it with you."

The next instant the savages were upon them. One of the red warriors raised his hatchet aloft to crush John's skull; but Dan was too quick for him, and springing before the body of his friend, he gave the savage a blow between the eyes with his fist, that sent him reeling to the ground. A shout of laughter from the Indians, who now came running up, greeted this exploit, and the one who seemed to be the leader of the party called out to his men not to kill the prisoners. They were seized, however, and bound securely. One of the Indians then examined John's wound in the leg, and after chewing up some leaves which he took from his belt, bound them tightly around the hurt. The pursuit of the other whites was now abandoned, and the Indians told the young men by signs that they must go with them. This the captives prepared to do, and the party set off in the direction of the river. It was too high to be forded, but the savages had two large canoes concealed on the Virginia shore, and by means of these they were soon on their own soil again. The canoes were drawn up and concealed in the woods, and the band set off for their towns in the north-western part of Ohio. They camped about dark, and their prisoners were bound hand and foot, to keep them from escaping. The cords were tied so tight as to be painful, and the young men could scarcely sleep at all. They were thankful when the morning came, and the march was resumed. John's leg was very painful, but the savages forced him to keep up with them, in spite of this. Dan walked by him all the way, often supporting him, and sometimes almost carrying him. He was always cheerful, and inclined to take a hopeful view of matters, and his devotion to his wounded friend, for whose sake he had suffered himself to be captured, was beautiful to behold.

On the morning of the fifth day the savages halted in about two hours after breaking up their camp of the previous night. They painted themselves hideously, and then, approaching their prisoners, smeared the face of each with a black substance. John's heart sank within him at this, for he knew that it was a sign that they were doomed to death, and his knowledge of the Indian customs told him what kind of death they were appointed to die. The savage who painted him must have read this in the young man's face, for he burst into a brutal laugh as he smeared the dye over the skin. John looked at Dan in silence. The young man's face was pale, but tranquil, and he met John's look with a smile.

"What is it?" he asked.

"I don't mind it for myself, Dan," said John, in a trembling voice, "but I can't bear to think that you should be here on my account."

"Well, then, don't think of it," said Dan. "To tell the truth, John, I don't care to live after you are gone. We've been together so long that to lose you would be like giving up a part of myself."

The savages now resumed their walk, and the two friends were ordered to move on.

About noon the Indians gave two loud whoops of a peculiar character, which were meant to let all their people within hearing know that they had returned with two prisoners. The whoops were repeated twice, at intervals of half an hour, and, the third time, were answered some distance in advance. Then was heard a furious barking of dogs, and in a short time a bend in the road brought them in sight of an Indian village of some fifteen or twenty wigwams, or lodges. The savage that had painted the prisoners now turned to them, and pointed exultantly to their paint and then to the lodges, as much as to say they had reached the place where they were to die.

CHAPTER XII.

THE TORTURE.

THE town to which the two friends were carried by their captors belonged to a tribe of Mingo Indians, and was situated about half way between Wheeling and Lake Erie. It consisted of about fifteen or twenty huts, or lodges, and contained a population of about one hundred souls, of whom thirty were warriors. It was one of the remnants of that once powerful tribe which has been immortalized by the eloquence of Logan. The place was dirty and squalid-looking, and it was evident that the tribe was very poor.

The warriors were received at the entrance of the town by those who had remained at home, and by their women and children. The latter at once commenced to pelt the captives with mud and stones, and one old squaw struck

Dan in the face with a stick. Unable to resist the impulse, Dan gave her a box on the ear with his open hand, and sent her reeling from him. He expected to be killed or beaten for his audacity, but the savages burst into a laugh at the discomfiture of the squaw, and ordered her to let the prisoners alone. After this, John and Dan were taken to one of the lodges, and after being tied hand and foot, were forced to lie down upon the ground, and a guard was placed at the entrance of the hut. About nightfall they were given some coarse, boiled hominy, and their hands were released until they had finished their meal. Then they were tied again, and forced to lie down on the floor of the hut. The night, which was a sleepless one to them, was passed by their captors in drinking and carousing, and they could hear their savage laughter until near daybreak, after which everything grew quiet.

"What do you think they will do with us, John?" asked Dan, who had been lying very still.

"They will burn us, without doubt," replied his companion. "We shall know to-morrow, however."

The next day at noon they were taken from their place of confinement, and carried into the open square of the town. A large fire was built in the centre of the space, and around it the oldest warriors were seated, smoking. The prisoners were placed before this group, and the remainder of the tribe stood by in silence to hear the result of the deliberations. One of the smokers arose, and, removing his pipe, commenced a long address, in the course of which he became very much excited, and pointed frequently and angrily to the captives, who stood by, unable to comprehend his language, but clearly understanding that he was urging his companions to put them to death.

At length the man sat down, and there was a profound silence. No one raised his voice for mercy to the captives. In a few moments the chief, who sat at the head of the smokers, took a large knife, and cut a notch on the side of his club. The knife and club were then passed around the circle of smokers, each of whom cut a notch in the wood. This was the Indian method of deciding the fate of the captives, for each notch was a vote in favor of their death. Had there been any present who desired to be merciful, he would have passed the club to his neighbor without cutting it. After the club had gone around the circle, it was handed back to the chief, who counted the notches, and then rose and announced the decision of the council. The prisoners were doomed to die at the stake at sunrise the next day.

One of the old warriors, who could speak a little English, then informed the prisoners of their sentence. He told them that they would now have to run the gantlet of the warriors of the tribe, and that, although the council had condemned them to death, they would be spared upon condition of their joining the tribe, if they could succeed in reaching the end of their terrible journey without being knocked down by the clubs of the warriors.

The savages were then ranged in two rows, facing each other, about three or four feet apart, and each one was armed with a stout club. The prisoners were then placed at one end of the rows, and ordered to run at full speed to the lower end of the line, and then return. Dan Whittaker was the first to start, and for a while he was successful in dodging the blows which were aimed at him; but at length a large Indian struck him fairly over the head, and laid him bleeding upon the ground. John was not more fortunate. His wound prevented him from running, and he had gone but a few steps when he was knocked senseless. The savages then dragged the poor fellows back to the lodge in which they had spent the previous night, and left them there with a guard, to recover their consciousness as best they could.

Dan was the first to recover. He raised himself up, and, seeing John still insensible, crawled over to him, and, supporting his head in his lap, tried to restore him to consciousness. At last he was successful. As John opened his eyes, and saw his faithful friend bending over him, he put up his arms, and, clasping him around the neck, drew him down to him.

"God bless you, Dan," he whispered. "I think we can die more bravely together than either of us could apart."

"I know it, John," said Dan.

They spent the rest of the day and the night in talking of home and those they loved. This seemed to comfort them, although the thought that they would never see home or friends again was bitter enough to them. Both of them had been raised by Christian parents, and they had lived the few years of their lives as becomes those who "profess the faith of Christ crucified;" and in these dark hours they found this faith as weet solace and a powerful support. As the night waned and the day dawned, they sang the hymns they had sung at home, until the lodge was filled with the melody, and even the savages, roused from their slumbers, listened with awe to what they thought the death-song of the pale-faces.

At sunrise the town was astir, and soon after, the Indians came to conduct their prisoners to the place of torture. The place selected for the occasion was the spot where the council had been held and the sentence passed on the previous day. Two stout posts had been driven into the ground, about three feet apart, and around them a quantity of fagots had been piled up. The prisoners were halted at the stakes, and stripped to the skin. Their hands were then tied behind them, and they were led to the posts, and fastened there by stout thongs of untanned buffalo hide. Even the savages seemed touched by the devotion of the two friends to each other, for they did not offer to separate them, as they embraced each other for the last time, but patiently waited till their parting was ended.

"Remember, Dan," said John, as they were bound to the posts, "we must die like men. Not a word, not a groan, must show these monsters how we are suffering. The Lord will sustain us, and we shall meet again in another and a better world, never to part there."

"Never to part there, never to part," repeated Dan. The savages now formed a ring around the stakes, and commenced to dance around them, keeping time to a wild, piercing chant. This was continued for a quarter of an hour, when they fell back, and half a dozen warriors advanced, with small bows and a number of fine needles, or arrows, of fat pine, which they commenced to shoot into the naked bodies of their victims. These arrows caused painful wounds wherever they struck, and started the blood in little, fine streams. After shooting about a dozen of these arrows into each of the victims, the men fell back, and an old squaw advanced with a burning torch, to fire the pile of fagots and light the pine arrows which were sticking in the quivering flesh of the young men.

The town was built just on the edge of the woods, and the stakes were not more than fifty or sixty yards from the trees. Every member of the tribe had assembled to witness the torture, and the red-skins were collected in a close knot in front of the stakes, in order to obtain a view of the prisoners' faces, and were standing with their backs to the woods. As the old woman advanced towards the pile, a sheet of flame and smoke, accompanied by a terrific crash, burst from the woods in the rear of the savages, and a storm of bullets swept through their midst, cutting down a number of warriors and women and children. The next moment a large force of hunters dashed out of the forest with a yell, and rushed upon the savages with the tomahawk. The surprise was complete. The Indians were utterly unprepared for and unsuspicious of such an attack; and, though they made a gallant resistance, they were put to flight, with the loss of half their tribe. The whites were merciless, and they spared neither age nor sex. They had come out for the purpose of avenging the injuries they had suffered, and they were resolved to exterminate the savages.

True to her instincts, the squaw had tried to fire the pile in spite of the attack; but a blow from the hatchet of one of the whites deprived her of life and the power of doing so. The captives were instantly released, the arrows were drawn from their bodies, and their wounds were dressed by their rescuers as tenderly and carefully as if the battle was not raging around them. The clothing of which they had been stripped was lying on the ground near the stakes, and they were soon clad in their own garments again. In answer to their questions, the men who had come to their assistance told them that the expedition consisted of one hundred men. It had been organized at Wheeling, under the command of Major Samuel McCulloch, the famous Indian-fighter. It had been intended for service in another quarter; but the old hunter, Bill Davis, had come in haste to Fort Henry, and begged Major McCulloch to help him to rescue "his boys," as he called John and Dan. McCulloch had generously consented to do this, and by a forced march of two days and nights had reached the town just in time to save them.

In half an hour the savages were routed with terrible slaughter, and the battle was over. Major McCulloch now approached the young men, who were resting on the ground stiff and sore from their wounds and bruises. They rose as he came up to them, and, grasping both his hands, thanked him warmly for their rescue.

"You don't owe me anything," he said. "I am fully repaid for my part of the trouble by seeing you safe. Your thanks are due to your friend Davis, for he fairly dragged us here. Where is he? I haven't seen him since the fight began."

One of the men approached, and, touching John on the shoulder, said, —

"Bill Davis has been badly wounded, and wants to see you."

Leaning on Dan's arm, John limped after the man, and Major McCulloch, who was an old friend of the hunter, followed anxiously. They found the old man lying on the ground just on the outskirts of the village. He had been shot through the breast at the opening of the fight, and was now very faint from loss of blood. He was lying with his eyes closed, and his breathing was labored and painful. John sank down by him, and, clasping his hand in both of his, called his name in a tone of sharp pain. The hunter opened his eyes, with a smile, at the sound of "his boy's" voice.

"So you've come, lad," he said, faintly, "and we got here in time to save you."

"Yes, Bill," said John, tearfully; "but at what a price! Are you hurt much?"

"I'm done for this time," said the hunter; "but I'm satisfied, so long as you are safe. Let me rest my head in your lap, lad, and I'll die easier then."

John lifted the old man's head into his lap, and his tears fell fast upon the worn, weather-beaten face. The men gathered around in silence, leaning on their rifles, and gazing with tender pity upon the scene.

"I wish I could die for you, Bill," John sobbed, as he stroked back the old man's hair, tenderly.

"It's better as it is, lad," said the hunter, faintly. "I'm an old fellow, and I've seen my day; so it doesn't much matter about me. You are young and vigorous, and you'll live to see the country peaceful and settled yet. But, lad, when you and Annie are married, and your little ones are playing at your knees, I want you to teach them the name of the poor old hunter that loved you so much; and if you would call one of them by my name, I think I shall know it, and be happier in that world where I am going; for I couldn't bear to die, if I thought you would forget me."

"I shall never forget you, Bill — never," said the young man, weeping. "None of my blood will ever cease to remember you."

"I know it," said the hunter, "and it is that that makes me willing to die; for if you had been my own flesh and blood, I couldn't have loved you more. Where's Dan?" he asked.

"Here I am, Bill," said Dan, controlling his emotion, and taking the old man's hand.

"Dan Whittaker," said the old man, "I have always loved you, too, because you loved John; but not like I loved him, Dan — not like I loved him; and now I'm going to leave him to you. You will watch over him, Dan, and be to him all that I meant to have been, had I been spared. Will you promise me that?"

"I will, and, with God's help, I will keep my promise," said Dan.

"That's right," murmured the hunter, faintly. "With God's help; you can do nothing without it. He has helped me many a time, and I'm trusting to his mercy now. I've tried to live a correct life, though I couldn't help cussin' when I got mad. I never injured any one, and I ain't afeard to die. Only don't let the Injuns git my har. Bury me in the thick woods, whar they won't find me; for I couldn't rest easy with my sculp a-swingin' to a red-skin's belt. Promise me that."

"I do promise," said John.

The hunter lay still and silent for a moment, and his face commenced to take a grayish hue. A tremor passed through his frame, and he whispered faintly, —

"John, lad, I'm going. Will you pray with me — the Lord's prayer, lad? You say it, and I'll repeat after you, as I used to do at my mother's knee when I was an innocent child."

John's voice was choked with sobs, and it was only by an effort that he faltered out the blessed words.

"Our Father," he began.

"Our Father," repeated the hunter, faintly, and with difficulty.

"Which art — "

"Which art — " the voice wavering and sinking to a mere whisper.

"In heaven — "

"In heaven," whispered the old man, a

smile, so sweet that it thrilled those who gazed upon it, stealing over his dark face. "In heaven," he whispered again — "in heaven;" and the voice died away into silence — a blessed silence, thank God; for the old hunter was in heaven with his "Father."

They carried the hunter with them a day's journey towards Wheeling, and buried him in the thick woods, and concealed his grave so that neither beast nor savage would ever find it. The Indian has passed away, the forest has been hewn down, and towns and cities have sprung up around that spot since then; but a truer, nobler heart than that of the old hunter has never throbbed beneath the blue skies of the west.

John and Dan were very sad during the march homeward; for, in spite of their joy at their own rescue, the death of their old friend wrung their hearts with the deepest grief they had ever known. Major McCulloch and his men respected their sorrow, and left them almost to themselves. Upon reaching Fort Henry, they managed to get word of their safety to their friends at Fish Creek; but they staid at Wheeling till John's leg was well enough to enable him to continue the journey home on horseback.

CHAPTER XIII.

JOHN'S WEDDING.

WHEN John and Dan returned to Fish Creek, they met with a welcome that more than repaid them for the sufferings they had experienced. It was some time before the wound in John's leg healed entirely, for it had been very much aggravated by his being compelled to accompany the Indians, and make the march with his rescuers on foot, so that the winter was far advanced before he abandoned his character of invalid. To tell the truth, he found it very pleasant to be nursed by Annie, for his mother had quietly resigned that task to her; and it was not without regret that he found himself entitled no longer to a sick man's privileges. He was impatient for the spring to come; for on the first day of May he was to make Annie Clarke his wife.

People married very young in those days; and the old proverb, "Whom we first love we seldom marry," would not have applied to the frontier; for, as a general rule, the pioneers married so young that they did not have time to find a second love. It cost little or nothing to take a wife. Any man who could build a cabin, and clear up and work a few acres of land, was in a position to marry; for the women of those days were not afraid of poverty and toil.

From the first, it was determined that the wedding (the first that had ever been projected in the settlement) should be a grand affair. One of the cabins in the fort had been assigned to the young couple, and, for several weeks previous to the appointed day, the women were busy in arranging it for them. John and Dan worked, too, with a will (for the former had not forgotten his boyish ingenuity), in making the furniture and such like little knick-knacks as they could think of; so that, when everything was finished, the "establishment" of the young couple was the admiration of the entire community. It was all very rough and plain, to be sure; but, then, dear reader, those for whom it was designed were *satisfied* with it. Some of you, no doubt, look forward, and very properly, too, to beginning life, when you marry, in a handsome "brick" or "brown stone," "with all the modern conveniences," and a full assortment of tasteful household furniture. God grant that your hopes may be realized; but I doubt if, after all, you will be any happier or better satisfied than were these young people with their log cabin, and rough pine and oak household goods. Invitations were sent to the various settlements for twenty miles around; and it was understood that everybody who could come would do so, whether they were acquainted with the bride and groom or not. There was very little ceremony on the border, and people had but little use for formal introductions.

On the day before the wedding, John Oxenford went to Grove Creek, accompanied by Dan

Whittaker and Tom Oxenford, to bring the parson down to Fish Creek. They were to return with the company from Grove Creek the next day, and the marriage was to be celebrated at high noon.

On the morning of the first of May, 1781, a goodly company left Grove Creek to attend the wedding, or frolic — for at that period the terms were synonymous. You would have stared, could you have seen them, dear reader. The men were dressed in shoe packs,* moccasons, leather breeches, leggings, and linsey hunting-shirts. Each man carried his hunting-knife at his belt, his powder-horn and shot-pouch at his side, and his rifle was slung across his shoulder. The ladies were dressed in linsey petticoats, and linsey or linen bed-gowns, coarse shoes, stockings, and cotton handkerchiefs. If they wore gloves, the material used was a coarse buck-skin. Of jewelry there was none, unless, perhaps, some one might have been so fortunate as to be the possessor of some old

* A leather shoe, without a sole, made like a moccason.

family relic or heirloom, at which their granddaughters of to-day would be very apt to turn up their noses. The horses were caparisoned with bridles of rough tanned leather, old saddles that had been mended until very little of the original article was left, and girths which were as frequently a piece of rope as a leathern strap. Yet these good people thought all this very fine, and they were as merry and free from care as it is possible to imagine. The only thing they feared was an attack from the Indians; but even this was worth risking for the fun that was in store for them.

The party left the fort with a cheer, and set off in single file for Fish Creek. John, of course, was the observed of all, and was the object of many a good-natured, but homely, jest. He tried very hard to maintain his gravity, but found it impossible to do so; and at last, abandoning the attempt, he became as merry as though he had not been going to his own wedding. The forest rang with the laughter of the joyous party; and as some of the girls looked upon the handsome face and manly figure of the bridegroom elect, they could not help wishing to themselves that they were to stand in Annie Clarke's place.

The fort at Fish Creek was reached by eleven o'clock, and the guests were at once admitted, and their horses provided for. A number of persons of both sexes had already arrived from other parts of the country, and one or two young people had even come from as far as Wheeling. There was no cabin in the fort large enough to hold the company, and the big storehouse had been fitted up for the occasion. This had an earthen floor; but it was considered quite as good for dancing as one of plank would have been.

At twelve o'clock the parson took his station in the middle of the floor, and the company grouped about him to witness the ceremony. The next moment, Captain Oxenford and his wife came in, followed by the bride and groom elect. Annie was dressed in her best homespun petticoat, which came to her ankles, and a bodice of old linen that Mrs. Oxenford had brought with her from the east. Her plump, pretty ankles were encased in yarn stockings of the brightest red, and her foot, which was the perfection of beauty, was fitted into a pair of Indian moccasons. Her hair was braided tastefully and simply, and in it she wore a spray of wild violets. John was dressed in his best hunting-shirt, his buck-skin breeches, linsey leggings, and a pair of Indian moccasons, which he had secured upon the occasion referred to in the last chapter. "A handsomer couple never stood before a parson," was the unanimous comment of those present. Every one in the settlement loved them, and all rejoiced in their happiness. In a few minutes the parson had "tied the knot," and had made John Oxenford and Annie Clarke man and wife. Then the fort rang with the cheers of the men, the women waved their handkerchiefs, and all crowded around the happy pair to offer their congratulations, and kiss the bride.

The marriage over, the women repaired to the cabin of Captain Oxenford to get ready the dinner which had been provided, and the men set the tables, which had been loaned by the various families of the fort, in the store-house. The bride and groom were as active as the others in these preparations, and by two o'clock the company were all seated around the festive board. The dinner was a down-right sensible meal, and consisted of beef, pork, fowls, venison, and bear-meat, roasted and boiled, with an abundance of cabbage, potatoes, and other vegetables. Seats were scarce, but the men were willing to stand. There was a deficiency of knives, too; but this was easily remedied. The family knives were given to the ladies, and the men made use of their scalping-knives.

Whiskey took the place of wine, but it was drank in moderation, for the men were very Bayards in their deference to the gentler sex, and no one thought of getting drunk in such company. The dinner was eaten with zest, and when it was over there was not enough left for a single meal for a person with a moderate appetite.

When the tables were removed, the floor was cleared, and the dancing began. Think of it, you who wait till half the night is over, before beginning your pastime; think of going to a ball at four o'clock on a May afternoon! The fiddler was mounted on a barrel, at one end of the room, and the first figure, which was always, in such cases, "a square four," was called. Then came the "jigging it off," in which the four would divide into couples, and end the set with a jig. Then followed the reels and jigs, which continued without slackening, until the fiddler was forced to throw up his bow from sheer exhaustion. A brief rest was allowed him, and he was ordered to begin afresh. As fast as the dancers became tired, their places were supplied from the lookers-on; and thus the dance went on, until the next day had fairly dawned.

At ten o'clock a deputation of young maidens

stole away the bride, and, flying with her across the yard to her new home, soon had her tucked away in the bed, and half an hour later, the bridegroom disappeared from the ball-room, in company with Dan Whittaker and several of his friends; and these young men performed for him the kind office of stowing him away by the side of his bride. Then they returned to the ball-room.

The fun grew merrier now. No one was allowed to sleep, and even the parson had to take his share in the reels and jigs. The good man was found, towards midnight, nodding in a corner of the room. The young people seized him by the arms, amidst shouts of laughter, and dragging him out on the floor, bade the fiddler play "Hang out till to-morrow morning," in token that the parson would not be allowed to seek the rest he craved until the night was over; but he outwitted the revellers, however, and, taking refuge in the loft of one of the stables, slept there soundly from midnight till sunrise.

About two o'clock in the morning, some one called out to Captain Oxenford, —

"I say, cap', it's about time to send 'Black Betty' to the young folks."

Now, "Black Betty" was nothing more nor less than a bottle of corn whiskey, and it was the custom to send it to the newly-married pair towards the wee hours of the morning. This time "Betty" did not go alone, but the deputation that carried her took with them a supply of cabbage, pork, potatoes, and bear-meat, plentiful enough to feed the whole settlement, and the bride and groom were compelled to eat heartily of these provisions, although they protested that they were not hungry. The etiquette of the times supposed that they were famished.

The dancing ceased at sunrise, and the guests prepared to depart. By nine o'clock, after having partaken of a hearty breakfast, they were all on their homeward way, and the fort relapsed into its usual quietness.

John and Annie Oxenford lived to a good old age, and had the happiness of seeing the country settled and prosperous. In his seventieth year, the former redeemed the promise of his childhood, and built him a fine house where his father's cabin had first been located — the fort having been broken up, and the settlers scattered, after the close of the Indian wars. He lived to see his great-grandchildren at his knee, and to give the name of the old hunter, Bill Davis, — which was also that of his eldest son and grandchild, — to the first great-grandchild, so that to this day it is borne by his descendants.

Dan Whittaker married Mary Oxenford two years after John's marriage, and he and his wife died a few years before John. The friendship which the two men bore each other never wavered, and it was grief for the loss of Dan that helped to bring John Oxenford to his grave.

The descendants of those who formed the little settlement are still scattered through the country about Fish Creek; and to this day they cherish, as a sort of precious legacy, the traditions which their fathers handed down to them of the exploits of the *Pioneer Boys in Planting the Wilderness.*

www.ingramcontent.com/pod-product-compliance
Lightning Source LLC
LaVergne TN
LVHW010242110826
845151LV00004B/1368

* 9 7 8 1 4 2 5 5 2 3 5 8 9 *